ii

Letting Go

Len Joy

You don't drown by falling in the water.

You drown by staying there.

—ED COLE

Cover designed by Creative Designs, LLC

This book is a work of fiction. Names, characters, places, and incidents either are products of the author's imagination or are used fictitiously. Any resemblance to actual persons, living or dead, events, or locales is entirely coincidental.

Printed in the United States of America

ISBN: 978198107491

INTRODUCTION

I

t took me eight years, nine months and three days to write my first novel, *American Past Time.* My second novel, *Better Days,* will be released in the fall of 2018. I'm not sure how long that one took, but less than eight years.

When I had trouble working on those novels I would write short fiction pieces. I am grateful to all of those folks who produce literary fiction journals. Especially the ones who published my stories. Producing a literary journal is a true labor of love.

Someone asked me what the theme of my collection was. I hate those questions. I'm really bad at theme. I don't think about a theme when I'm writing the story. I'm just trying to tell a story that interests me (and hopefully someone else). I decided I could at least come up with a tagline for each story and maybe that would reveal to me a central theme of my work.

Here's a few of them:

"Riding a Greyhound Bus into the New World" – a widower searches for the innocent boy he used to be;

"Dalton's Good Fortune" – a down-on-his luck ex-soldier gets a new perspective on his life from a fortune teller;

"This Train Makes all the Stops" – a man tries to adapt to a new world after his wife dies;

"Letting Go," – a woman in an emergency room waiting for word on her husband, reflects on her marriage;

Most of the stories are about people who have lost something and are trying to find a way to move on with their lives. I hope you enjoy them.

Len Joy

May 10, 2018

CONTENTS

To the Zoetrope Online Writers Workshop created by Francis Ford Coppola. This community of writers has provided a nurturing, creative environment for hundreds of aspiring writers for over a decade.

RIDING A GREYHOUND BUS INTO THE NEW WORLD

O n the second day of my married life, I found myself sitting next to Edgar Rawlings in the back seat of a Greyhound Bus bound for Montreal. I was on my honeymoon. Edgar was returning to prison. It was snowing.

My first day in this new world hadn't gone so well. It was my wedding day and I'd left Crystal's ring at my parent's house on Long Island. When I told her, she tried to give me her angry look, but she couldn't pull it off and started giggling. She would tell the "Joel forgot my wedding ring" story for the next thirty years. She thought she was so funny. Crystal died last year.

Forgetting the ring unnerved me but was nothing compared to how I felt when her father asked me about our honeymoon plans.

"We're driving to Montreal. Staying at the Hotel Bonaventure," I said. Her father was tall, grey, and imperious. I unfolded my roadmap on his desk and showed him how I'd red-penciled our route. He didn't even look at it.

"Joel, how the hell are you going to drive to Montreal? Don't you know they aren't selling gas on weekends?"

It was December 1973. I was aware of the energy crisis in sort of an academic way, but in grad school we never drove anywhere. I stood in his den, clutching my stupid map, my face burning. I was going to be married in three hours and had already screwed up our honeymoon.

He tossed me a phonebook. "Call Greyhound."

We spent our wedding night at the local Holiday Inn, overslept, and nearly missed the bus. Crystal squeezed into a window seat next to a woman who had to weigh three hundred pounds. She winked at me and started writing thank you notes.

1

I found a seat in the last row, next to a skinny kid in green workpants and a baggy flannel shirt.

He moved his bag. "Here partner, take a load off." He patted the seat. "I was hoping they'd oversell and bump me. Get to extend my furlough." He held out his hand. "Name's Edgar Rawlings."

We shook hands. "I'm Joel. You're a soldier?" I asked.

"Nah. Prison furlough. Trustee's meeting the bus at Napier to drive me back."

Edgar had a rough buzz-cut and the hint of whiskers on his chin and upper lip. He opened his sack and took out a croissant. He pushed the bag towards me, "My mom baked them."

I wondered if there were rules about eating on the bus, but didn't want to offend him. "These taste awesome, Edgar," I said, my mouth full.

His face lit up. "Where you headed, Joel?"

When I told him I was going to Montreal on my honeymoon he nearly jumped out of his seat. "Montreal's the greatest city in the world. I know a place has rolls almost as good as Mom's. Let me borrow your pen."

I reached for the silver Cross pen in my shirt pocket. Edgar ripped a piece of paper out of his notebook and wrote down the name of the bakery. "Ask for Mario. Tell him Edgar Rawlings sent you."

Turned out Edgar was a Yankees fan. When I told him I'd grown up on Long Island and had actually been to Yankee Stadium he pumped me for information. What was Billy Martin like? What did I think of Winfield? Did I ever see Mickey Mantle play? When the bus stopped in Napier, I couldn't believe we'd been talking for two hours.

"Good luck, Edgar." I stood up and shook his hand.

"You and your girl gonna love Mario's." As he reached the bus door he looked over at Crystal, still shoehorned into her seat, and gave me a thumbs-up. He didn't act like someone going back to prison. He didn't act like he'd been in prison. He was just a kid, like me.

I watched him stroll towards a rusty van parked near the bus. The driver, a bear of a man with greasy matted hair and a beard, got out. He pushed Edgar up against the vehicle and frisked him. Then he shoved him into the back of the van and marched over to the bus driver who was smoking a cigarette at the curb. The bus driver shrugged and lit another cigarette as the van driver boarded the bus and headed down the aisle to my seat. "This your pen?" he asked.

He was holding my Cross pen. My hand rose to my shirt pocket. "Uh...."

"That punk stole it from you. Damn stupid thing to do."

I could tell Edgar was in big trouble. "It's not my pen," I blurted.

2

"What...?"

"I gave it to him for, uh...his croissants."

"Sure you did." He wrinkled up his face and poked the pen into my pocket like I was a grade-schooler. "Cons can't have fancy college-boy pens. Might make a shiv. Hurt someone. Wouldn't want that on your do-gooder conscience."

He wheeled around and stomped off the bus. As we headed off down that highway I looked out the window at the van taking Edgar back to prison. I wondered what would happen to him. He was a good guy.

So was Joel. Somewhere on that highway he got lost. Some days I forget he ever existed. But on these cold lonely nights when snow covers my world, I miss that boy.

TRIAGE

Frank Summers wandered into his garage in search of a project. After thirty years as an emergency room surgeon at Phoenix General, he'd been forced to retire when PG was gobbled up by one of those hospital corporations run by accountants.

In his first month of retirement he'd swum a thousand laps in his pool, mastered thirty new iPhone apps, read five forgettable novels and played one round of golf with his wife, Lilly.

Car keys in hand, Lilly entered the garage. "What are you doing out here, Frank?" Her blondish hair was ponytailed and she was wearing jeans and a tee-shirt. Her animal shelter uniform.

Lilly, who'd retired ten years ago, had been no more excited about Frank's retirement than Frank. She played golf three days a week, volunteered at the shelter on weekends, and took writing classes at the college. She was busier than when the kids were at home. And happier. Frank didn't want to interfere with her life.

"I thought I'd clean the garage."

She wrinkled her nose. "In this heat? Do something fun." She pointed to the mountain bikes hanging from the ceiling. "Take Frank Jr.'s bike. You can ride along the canal all the way to 75th Avenue."

"Good idea. I haven't been on those mountain preserve trails in years."

"Not the trails, Frank. The bike path. Leave the saguaros for the kids."

Frank cruised through the mountain preserve on the novice trail that circumnavigated the mountains. Not as exciting as the ER, but it beat the hell out of golf. Two girls passed him and took the intermediate trail that branched off to the right. Frank followed them. He missed his nurses. The close quarters of the operating room. The camaraderie. The not-so-innocent touches.

The trail got rougher – pebbled with chunks of white granite and guarded by bottle cacti and some distant saguaros. It was high noon, blistering hot and eerily quiet. Everyone had gone home – even the birds. He rounded a large outcropping and headed downhill, with mountainside to his left and steep valley to his right. He tugged on his helmet strap, then squeezed the brakes.

It was a rush. His heart beat wildly as the bike careened down the rocky pathway. And then the image of Inez in her hot tub – her bronze breasts and brown nipples luminous in the foamy water – popped into his head, uninvited. She'd been his last ER nurse.

A bowling-ball chunk of granite loomed in the center of the trail. Frank steered hard to his left, but the bike fishtailed into the wall, shot back across the path, hit another rock and went airborne.

Frank lost his grip and hurtled into space.

His son's twenty-year old helmet smashed into the mountainside and split like a walnut, but when Frank stopped bouncing fifty feet below the edge of the trail he was still conscious. The helmet had done its job. Frank wouldn't die from a head injury. However, as he assessed his situation, he found little reason for optimism. His palms had been filleted, his right ankle severely sprained and he had at least four broken ribs, one of which had punctured his lung. With the stifling heat and the oozing wounds he figured he had three hours, tops.

The bike with his iPhone and water were a hundred feet farther down the mountainside. The trail ledge was closer, but with his hands nearly useless, he couldn't climb. He rolled over. The broken rib stabbed his lung. He took shallow breaths and when his heart stopped racing he rolled over again.

It took him two hours to reach his bike. His water bottle was missing. He unsnapped the seatbag with his teeth and coaxed the iPhone out of its pocket.

No bars.

Fucking retirement really sucked.

He closed his eyes, then remembered the pictures. He pressed his bloody fingertip on the photo app and opened the Nurses folder.

Crazy Kelly on her boat.

Bonita flashing her snake tats.

Wendy giving him the finger.

Karen.

Sami.

Rebecca.

Inez in all her hot-tub glory.

One last look, then he deleted the folder.

He opened the family album and thumbed to the photo of Lilly and him on the beach at Malibu.

So young. So happy. So in love.

He kissed the screen and propped the phone on a rock so he could see it as he lay on the mountainside.

MY FATHER'S ICE

I have come to the Whitney Museum today to find Harry Giles. Not the wealthy investment banker with the beautiful socialite wife. Not the man who read "Goodnight Moon" to his daughter every night. I want to learn about the young man who dropped out of Cornell to follow his hero to an abandoned Brooklyn tenement in the pursuit of art. What happened to that boy who would become my father?

Last week my mother, not the most sentimental of women, sent me a photograph from her prom. She was decluttering and this cheesy relic didn't make her cut. She'd attached an annoying post-it note: "Carly – Look at that hemline!!!" Mother loves her exclamations.

The photographer naturally focused on my mother, blonde and sunny in a red mini-dress, with her perfect swimsuit-model body. My father stands off to the side, looking uncomfortable in his rented tux. It doesn't matter. No one's going to notice him.

I am my father's daughter. Dark. Anxious. My smile always a heartbeat too late for the camera's flash.

Today I've decided to attend the Whitney's exhibition of my father's hero: renegade architect, Gordon Matta-Clark. Mother is not pleased.

"Gordon's been dead thirty years, Carly. Why waste your time?"

Sometimes I imagine telling my mother what I really think.

"You know the difference between you and me, Mom?"

In my imaginary world she waits for my answer.

"You never understood why Dad ran off to New York, and I never understood why he came back."

The exhibition is showing a documentary from 1974.

Matta-Clark uses his chainsaw to transform a Brooklyn tenement into a three-story sculpture. As he carves a hole, a boy emerges from the shadows, holding a floodlight. Shirtless, body slick, lips pressed tight.

I have seen that look before.

6

I remember the day we moved from cozy Skokie to snooty Winnetka.

My father was in the den packing his photographs of Gordon's work. He was studying one of them, but it wasn't a building sculpture.

It was a photo of him with his arm draped around a curly-haired girl. Next to them, a long-haired man with a bad complexion.

"Gordon?" I asked, pointing to the blotchy-faced man.

He smiled. "Yes."

"Who's that lady?"

There was a slight pinch around his eyes. "We worked together. She died."

He shoved the picture in with the others and wrote "ATTIC" on the packing carton.

Matta-Clark stops the chainsaw. The curly-haired girl sweeps. The boy with the light moves closer and says something. She laughs.

The summer after we moved, my parents hosted a lawn party for the firm's newest class of MBAs. While father grilled, Mother entertained with her story of how Mr. Giles started with the firm.

"Harry took a most unusual path. Fell in with a bad crowd and abandoned his studies." She smiled indulgently as the MBAs looked skeptical. "It's true. He joined an avant-garde artiste-troupe. They vandalized abandoned buildings."

The MBAs laughed nervously. I wanted my father to tell them the truth, but he just shrugged and offered the young acolytes his faux-smile.

I took art in high school to annoy my mother.

"Colleges will not take you seriously," she said.

I wanted to tell her I didn't care, but instead I tacked into the fierce wind of her displeasure. "They're for extra credit, Mom."

Then I discovered fashion and pursued it passionately, ignoring my mother's disdain. One day I showed my designs to my father.

"These are special, Carly. Gordon would have been impressed."

He could offer no higher praise.

"I'm sorry his buildings got torn down," I said.

He shrugged. "Nothing lasts, Carly."

Pratt, in Brooklyn, offered me a full scholarship. Mother wasn't pleased.

"Fashion is not the life you want. Trust me."

She was certain Pratt was a mistake. I was certain of nothing. In a battle of wills – a huge mismatch. I needed father's help.

He was studying financials at the ornate teak desk Mother and her decorator had selected for his den.

"Mom's not thrilled with Pratt," I said.

He put down his documents. "She doesn't think it's practical," he said.

"You wanted to be an architect. Was that practical?"

He smiled sadly. "I met Gordon at Cornell. He was a guest professor for a term. He made architecture exciting. When he asked me to come to New York, I didn't think twice."

"Where was Mom?"

He grimaced. "Back in Chicago, waiting for us to get married. I worked with Gordon for a year. Then he got a commission in London. I couldn't go with him."

"Why?"

He shook his head. "Ancient history. I came home, got married and your grandfather offered me a job with the firm."

"But you wanted to be an architect?"

"He assigned me to Stanley Wiggins – serious rainmaker. Stanley told me a few years and I'd have enough money I could do whatever I wanted."

He pushed his chair back. "The world doesn't work that way. I know that now."

"One late winter day, Stanley decides that instead of eating lunch at his desk, he'll walk to his club." My father walked over to the coffee table and picked up a glass paperweight. "A chunk of ice, no bigger than this," he held the paperweight above his head, "dislodges from Hancock Tower and crushes Stanley's skull."

He lowered his arm and set the paperweight back on the table.

"I replaced Stanley. Dollars fell on me. I couldn't leave."

My father's ice was a small blood-clot, the size of a pea, which dislodged from his heart and found its way to his carotid artery where it blocked the blood to his brain. In the battle between his good heart and his brilliant mind, that was the only time his heart won.

He died a month before I started at Pratt.

At the exit, one of Matta-Clark's home movies is playing. Gordon talking to a group of rowdy conventioneers. Suddenly the camera zooms to a table in the corner.

A young man clasps the hands of a freckle-splashed girl with a tangle of curly red hair. I hold my breath. She has dark eyes and full lips. Her arms have a comforting fleshiness as she wraps them around the boy. They kiss. A lingering, gentle kiss. When their lips part, the boy turns towards the camera.

His face is radiant and his thirty year old moment of happiness fills the screen and bathes me in its glow.

8

FIFTEEN MINUTES

Back in sixty-two, before the drugs and the booze and the wives had taken everything he had to offer the world, the Kennedys had been his private guests, staying with him at his compound on the Island. Jackie had found him tres amusant, and at dinner Jack had finished off his last bottle of Chateau Mouton Rothschild (the 1933 vintage – before everything went to hell). But when he died last week at the age of ninety-five, he rated just three lines on page fifty-six of The Times, a death notice not an obituary – written, no doubt, by someone who had never heard of him, and read, no doubt, by folks who thought he had died long ago.

MARY BRYAN CAKE

I sit down by my mother on her TV-watching couch – the only furniture we kept when I moved her into the efficiency unit at Cedar Rest. Dr. Phil is hectoring some poor schlub who cheated with his wife's sister. I grab the remote and mute him.

Mom gives me a look.

I hand her the photo album I found buried under forty years of her National Geographics. "Dayton – 1965" is stenciled across the cover.

She frowns. "Why were you in my basement?"

My mother and I have spent a lifetime not talking about the stuff that matters. I'd been cleaning out her house so I can sell it to pay for Cedar Rest. She doesn't want to hear that. And she probably doesn't want to talk to about that last family vacation, either.

For generations my father's family worked at the Goodyear plant in Dayton. His two older brothers followed the plan, but not my father. He didn't like people telling him what to do. He took over a drive-in theatre up in Lansing, where he met Mom. Six months after I arrived the drive-in folded. We moved to Amarillo and he bought a muffler shop just before Midas opened down the block. His last shot – a full-service carwash in Bakersfield – had a couple good years until the self-service places started showing up everywhere.

My mother glances at the first page and shakes her head. "Your father's grand 4th of July expedition."

After the carwash closed he had to take a job at Sears. Normal hours, paid vacation and a twenty percent discount on equipment. He hated it. With his discount he bought a movie camera and with the vacation he drove us across the country to visit his brothers back in Ohio. I was twelve years old that summer – the year before my father killed himself.

His snapshots traced our route. Mom and I squeezed into a booth at the Waffle House in Barstow. Me standing at attention by the entrance to Roman Nose State Park in Oklahoma. An inexplicable line of customers queued up to enter a Bob Evans sausage emporium in Indiana. And then pages and pages of Dayton's 4th of July Parade. I didn't remember any of it.

"No pictures of Dad?" I ask.

Mom shrugs. "His camera." She snortles at the last photo, which fills the back page. It's the whole clan – Dad's brothers, Nick and Tony, and their wives and kids, with Mom hidden in the back as though she didn't belong. I'm front and center with the Super 8, filming my father as he takes our picture.

How could I have forgotten that? The Sears camera he let me play with because he couldn't bring himself to use it. I filmed everything. "What happened to our home movies, Mom?"

She sucks in her cheeks like she used to do when she threaded a needle. "I threw them away during one of my angry decades. Sorry."

I shrug back at her.

"Who's that girl?" I point to a pensive blonde about my age.

Mom smiles. "That's Mary Bryan. She was a friend of one of your cousins."

"The Mary Bryan?" I ask. Every birthday while I was growing up my mother made a fabulous double fudge chocolate cake she called Mary Bryan Cake.

"She gave me the recipe."

In my mind I hear the clicky-clack of the film as it spools through the projector and I watch as my mother and father sit together eating Mary Bryan cake. My mother schmooshes her piece into my father's mouth like she's a new bride and all the aunts and uncles and cousins cheer as my father picks up my mother and kisses her with chocolate-frosting smeared lips.

THE GIRL FROM YESTERDAY

My boob job cost me three thousand nine hundred and ninety-nine dollars at Dr. Gupta's New You Clinic in Rolla. It was worth every penny. These boobs changed everything. I was a gawky six-footer with mousy brown hair and flat as a board. The only guy who ever paid me any mind was Wayne, and turned out Wayne was an asshole.

He got me pregnant when we were in high school. Check that. Tina, my best friend, says, Annie, you shouldn't say he got you pregnant, like you were some kind of spectator. So okay, Tina, WE got pregnant. Wayne didn't want to marry me (I think he always dreamed that one day he'd wake up handsome and find himself a prettier girl), but his father made him. His daddy's a crankgrinder over at the Caterpillar plant, same place I work.

We got married just before my eighteenth birthday. Little Wayne came along and then Ariel two years later. My mom was sixteen when she had me. She never talked about my father, except to say he wasn't from around here. She's been a cashier at the Foodliner for twenty-five years. She says you can tell a lot about a person from their groceries. Said she had her doubts about Wayne even before he knocked me up. He'd come in the store every day to buy a two-pack of Little Debbie chocolate cupcakes. Never switched, even when the Foodliner was practically giving away their Twinkies. Boy had no sense, she said. I had to admit that was Wayne through and through. He'd find something he liked – TV show, beer, sexual position – and that was that. Imagination wasn't his strong suit.

After Ariel was born, Wayne joined the National Guard. Said it was to make some extra money, but that wasn't true. He thought it was a great gig. Every month a weekend out of town, beer money from the government for driving a truck around with a bunch of other hillbillies, and a chance to try his luck with those girls that hung around Fort Leonard Wood. Didn't work out like he planned. They called up the Guard, and he got his ass sent to Iraq.

Right after he shipped out, my granny died and left me five thousand dollars. I didn't tell Wayne. After the funeral, I was over at my mom's and she had a copy of the West Plains Bugle. On the back page right there with the ads for liposuction and how to lose ten pounds in ten days I saw "Dr. Gupta's Breast Enhancement Special." I was a B cup, so I enhanced myself up to a double D.

Then I fixed my hair. Went to Monique's Salon in Springfield and got a razored shag and changed the color from mousy to platinum. Stopped at the mall and bought a bunch of new tops. I was transformed.

A month later I met Tina. I was in the parking lot of Graham's Country Station over near West Plains, screaming at Kit Rollins as he peeled out of the parking lot. Kit had brought me to the bar, but dumped me when he ran into his old high school girlfriend. And then it started to rain. A freezing, stick-to-your-skin Missouri rain. I was about to become an ice statue when Tina pulled up in her little old Camry and told me to get in the car.

Tina's a mail carrier and has to deal with all sorts of situations. She said I wasn't near as scary as Fred Tucker, who'd sit on his front porch in dirty boxers, scratching his balls, waiting for his disability check.

Me and Tina have been hanging out together ever since. Tina's over forty, but she has the cutest little-girl face, and a nice trim bod. I know lots of guys are interested, but she's pretty choosy. She'll give a guy one dance and then sit down.

We were having good times until a couple weeks ago when Wayne came home. He should have told me he was coming. Lanny George had given me a ride home from Jake's and we were fooling around when Wayne walked in on us. It looked worse than it was, but Wayne wouldn't listen. Called me a whore, wanted to fight Lanny, but he didn't push that. Wayne talks tough sometimes, but he's a pussycat.

He's back living with his dad for now. It was Tina's idea to change the locks. She said it was better to be safe than sorry. I guess she was right.

Tonight Tina picked me up at my mom's place where I had dropped off the kids.

Where should we go? she asked.

I said, How about Jake's?

Jake's is sort of a biker–hillbilly bar. Mostly locals. Tina didn't say anything, just did this thing with her lip, sort of a sneer, acting like she was too good for Jake's.

Hey. It's a fun place, I said. A family bar.

She said, Yeah if your old man's in the joint, or your mom's turning tricks, it's a great place for the family.

Sometimes Tina's a snob.

Well then, I said, it's a perfect place for you because all you do is make fun of people. You don't ever give any of these guys a chance.

So she gave me that look like she's my mother and said, Your problem, Annie, is you give everyone a chance. You fall for a line from guys like Kit or Lanny just because they ignored you in high school. Now you've got tits and they're all over you.

Not true, I said, but I didn't give her the finger or anything, like I would if I didn't sort of think she might be right.

You can do better. You're smart and funny. Don't settle for those losers, she said.

What about you? I said. Don't you ever want to meet someone? You like being alone?

The minute I said it, I wished I hadn't, cause she got all sad-faced and started concentrating real hard on her driving.

There are worse things than being alone, she whispered.

I decided she was probably right so I shut up.

We didn't talk the rest of the way to the bar. Jake's is a couple miles out of town. The parking lot is just a big field full of potholes and ruts. The front lot was packed with Harleys and pickups. Tina's Camry rocked through the potholes as she headed to the back.

Where you going? I asked.

She gave me a look. Said she thought the family parking was in the rear. We laughed and everything was okay again.

While we waited in line for the bouncer to check our IDs, Tina reminded me that she's on call so I might have to get my own ride home. She's an EMT – part of the Maple Springs volunteer fire department. She gave me her pep talk about how I shouldn't drink too much or run off and do coke with any of the patrons and she did this little air quotes thing when she said patrons, just in case I'd forgotten what she thought of Jake's customers.

We had hardly sat down at the bar in the back, when the guy next to me offered to buy us both drinks. Gregory or Randall, some fancy-boy name like that. He was a pretty boy. Dreamy blue eyes, with his hair all slicked back. He was too old to have ignored me in high school, which I took as a good sign. When he asked me to dance I said okay.

So me and GregoryRandall were dancing. Well I was dancing, he was moving like the Tinman, but with a leer. I didn't mind because I was looking good in my ruby-red basketball shorts and wifebeater. After every song the bar gal walked by with Jager shots and GregoryRandall kept pounding them down. They didn't improve his dancing. Tina came over and yelled in my ear that she'd been paged.

I gotta take off, she said. You're on your own. Don't fall in love tonight.

How am I going to get home? I asked.

Call a taxi. They're a lot cheaper than any of these guys, and she gave a look over at RandallGregory like he was a radioactive piece of shit, which it turned out he was.

14

Five minutes after Tina left, RG told me he wanted to go party. Grabbed my hand and started dragging me toward the door like I was his slave. I yanked my arm away and told him I wasn't interested. I headed back to my barstool and he grabbed me, all red-faced, like no chick had ever turned him down or something.

What's the deal? You saving yourself for your dyke friend?

She's hotter than you, pansy boy.

I sat down and tried to ignore him, but he grabbed my shoulder and spun me around.

You stupid bimbo, he said.

When I was a flat-chested brown-haired girl, nobody called me stupid, so I punched him in the nose. Turned out the pretty boy was a bleeder. I didn't hit him that hard, but he gushed blood. The guys at the bar laughed as the bouncer dragged RandallGregory away. Then he came back and told me I had to leave too. Same rules for chicks and guys.

I was out in front of Jake's hunting through my bag for my cellphone so I could call the Maple Springs taxi when I heard this deep voice behind me.

Need a ride, lady?

I turned around. It was this old guy I'd seen around the bar a few times. I remembered him because he was missing a bunch of fingers on one hand. I'd never heard him say anything before tonight.

Oh, I said, and stared at him like I really was a dumb blonde.

A ride. Do you need a ride? he asked again.

He stood ramrod straight, his arms at his sides, like he didn't know what to do with them. I was surprised – he was taller than me. I hadn't really looked at him close before. Probably cause of the hand. His face was all leathery, like boots after they get nice and broke in, and his hair was short, wheat-colored. He didn't look all that bad for an old guy.

My truck's over there, he said, pointing to the far end of the parking lot about three freaking miles away. Name's Doak. I'll give you a ride.

Annie, I said. Why you parked in the next county? You some sort of exercise nut?

Too many drunks around here, he said, and he sort of half smiled.

We started walking toward his pickup when Wayne's ugly purple truck bounced into the parking lot. He slammed on the brakes and jumped out. He was dressed like Johnny Cash – black cowboy shirt with mother of pearl snaps, black wranglers and silvered lizard-skin boots. Still had his army haircut though, and that sort of ruined the effect.

Hey, Annie baby, how ya doing? Taking gramps out for a walk? Didn't get a chance the other day to tell you how hot you look as a blonde. And those tits are awesome.

15

Just ignore him, I said.

Ignore who? Doak said.

Wayne stopped smiling. Listen old man, I got business to take care of with my lady, so get your sorry drunk ass out of here.

You're in our way, Doak said.

Our way? Fuck you.

And then Wayne punched Doak in the face. It surprised me because he's not a fighter. But my surprise was nothing compared to Wayne's. Doak didn't fall down. He sort of bent with the punch, like a pine tree whipped by a gust of wind, and then he snapped back.

That was a mistake, Doak said.

Wayne stepped back. He put up his fists and started bobbing up and down. A mistake? I'll show you a mistake, mister. He started bouncing up and down like he was Rocky Balboa.

Doak just stood there, hands still down by his sides, like he was bored. Wayne lunged at him and threw another punch. The next thing I knew Wayne was on the ground, screaming like a girl. He was holding his knee, yelling, He broke my fucking leg. That motherfucker broke my fucking leg.

Doak leaned over him. It ain't broke son. You'll be okay in a few minutes. Time to go, Annie.

We stepped around Wayne and got in Doak's truck. It was a twenty minute drive to my place and he didn't say ten words. His face was red and swolled up under his cheek, so I told him to come in so I could give him an ice pack.

Okay, he said.

Does it hurt? I asked.

We sat down on my couch and he held the ice pack on his cheek.

He wrinkled up his face. Ten years ago he wouldn't have landed that punch, he said. Nice place you got here. You got kids? He gave me that half-smile again. Wayne Jr. had left his trucks all over the living room, and Ariel had a dozen naked Barbies sleeping on the coffee table.

My mom's taking care of them tonight, I said. Sorry about the mess. The Wayne mess too.

He shook his head like it was nothing. He shifted on the couch trying to find a comfortable position.

What's the deal with Wayne, he asked.

So I told him about me and Wayne, even the part about getting caught with Lanny cause I didn't want to make it sound like I was some poor little victim.

You met him in high school? he asked.

16

I smiled, remembering how it felt to finally have a boyfriend. Wayne was a goofy kid, I said. Nobody paid him any mind. And I was this gawky giant, taller than all of the boys. We were a couple lonely losers.

What about your kids? he asked.

I love my babies. Wayne does too. But he wasn't ready. Wayne wanted to get laid, he didn't want to be a father. My mom always said that no father was better than a bad father.

She's right, he said.

You got kids, I asked?

Not anymore.

I waited for him to explain, but he just rubbed his jaw with his good hand and stared at me. I guess it was supposed to be my job to keep the conversation going.

Wayne looked sort of freaked when you were still standing after he hit you, I said.

There's an art to taking a punch, he said. Probably something you should know if you're going to keep getting in bar fights.

Show me, I said, and I patted his neck with a towel where the ice pack was dripping on him.

He put the ice pack down and turned to face me on the couch. He took my hands and made fists with them. Then he had me hold them up like I was a boxer.

When you see the punch coming, shorten your neck. Bring your shoulders up to brace yourself.

He slipped his hands into my armpits and pushed up my shoulders so I was sort of hunched up like a turtle hiding in its shell. He had a nice touch and he didn't even try to cop a feel.

Then the punch won't snap your neck.

He took his right hand, the one that had all its fingers, and he brought it up to my cheek, in a slow motion punch.

When you get hit, roll with the punch.

He took my face in his hands and gently twisted it away from where the punch would have landed.

Step back. Get your hands up to protect your face.

You didn't do that, I said. You just stood there like Wayne's punch was a mosquito bite.

I don't have a pretty face like you.

Nobody ever told me I was pretty. Not my mom. Not Wayne. No one.

I know another boxing move, I said.

Yeah?

I wrapped my arms around him and squeezed tight. My boobs pressed into his chest.

This is called a clinch, right?

I could tell he was trying to think of something to say. I kissed him. Hard. A real kiss. He kissed back. He was a good kisser.

I gave him a little love-bite on his earlobe.

You should have given the guy in the bar that lesson, I whispered.

Right. He didn't cover up and look what happened to him.

And his face was almost as pretty as mine.

I cupped my hands under my chin and batted my eyelashes, like I was some kind of southern belle. We both laughed. He had a nice laugh, sort of a surprise cause he looked so serious. I sat back on the couch and pulled my top off.

Do you want to fuck me? I asked.

His mouth dropped open, not like he was surprised, more like he was trying to catch his breath. The smile lines around his mouth twitched. He tried not to, but he couldn't keep his eyes from checking out my boobs. He reached around and unclasped my bra. We kissed and his good hand made little circles around my nipple. He broke the kiss and nuzzled my breasts.

You like? I asked.

You don't have to do this, he said.

What's wrong? You don't want me?

It's not that.

Well what?

I'm too old.

Come on, I said.

I took his hand and led him to my bedroom. He sat down on the bed. I pulled off his boots and he tugged off his jeans. He had tight, hard muscles in his arms and shoulders and a flat belly with no ass at all. In the shadows from the hall light, I could see the guy he used to be.

I slipped off my shorts and panties. I snuggled up next to him with my head on his chest. I could feel his heart thumping, slow and steady.

How old are your kids? he asked.

Wayne Junior is ten and Ariel is almost eight, I said.

I flipped over on top of him. He ran his hands down my back and kneaded my ass.

I saw that baseball glove on the floor. Does your boy play Little League? he asked.

All of sudden he's Mr. Small Talk.

18

That's Ariel's glove. Tina says Ariel is the Albert Pujols of the Landis Park T-Ball league.

He snorted. Not another Cardinal fan. Is Tina the gal that was at the bar with you tonight?

She's my best friend. Takes Ariel to her t-ball games when I work overtime. I started grinding on him and gave him a long deep kiss, figuring that would shut him up, but it didn't.

You work at the plant? he asked, when we came up for air.

I gave up and rolled over on my back.

Yeah, but I've been thinking about taking classes at the community college. Get my associates degree. Tina thinks I could become a nurse. She says I'm good with people. Especially old people, I said and I gave him a look.

He laughed. I guess she's right about that.

I climbed back on top.

I'll be sure to introduce you next time we go out, I whispered in his ear.

This time he kissed me. And then he started to rub my pussy. He had a nice touch. I stroked his cock and he got hard. I straddled him and he slid in easy. He cupped my breasts and we rocked back and forth slowly. His eyes were closed. His stub hand tickled my boob.

What happened to your hand? I asked.

He took his hand off my breast and looked at it like he'd never seen it before. Like it didn't belong to him. His cock went soft and slipped out, but he didn't seem to care.

Industrial accident, he said. He looked ten years older, like my question had drained the life out of him.

I started to say I was sorry, that I didn't mean to be nosy, when I heard a screech of tires. A few seconds later Wayne was pounding on the door, screaming my name.

Want me to talk to him? Doak asked.

No, I'll do it. I know how to handle him. He won't be any trouble, I said.

I didn't even bother to throw on my bathrobe. Just walked out and yelled at Wayne through the front door.

Wayne, stop the pounding.

Annie, let me in. I'm sorry babe. I'm sorry. Come on, let me in. I miss you, honey.

Go home. Don't make me call your father.

He stopped banging on the door. He was out of breath. He gasped for air, then he started to sob.

Wayne, just go home. We can talk tomorrow.

I heard him shuffle off, sniffling, but he must have spotted Doak's truck across the street, because he came back and started pounding again.

Are you screwing that old man, you cunt? How could you do that to me?

I'm calling the cops if you don't leave right now, Wayne.

Did he tell you how he lost his fingers? He tried to rip-off the Company. The sick fuck cut off his own motherfucking fingers, Annie!

Go home, Wayne!

He pounded the door one last time and then it was quiet. I heard the starter grind and then tires squealing as he raced off.

I walked back into the living room. Doak was dressed, standing in the middle of the room, hands dangling at his sides again, like when I met him.

Time to go, he said.

I didn't say anything, but I put my arms around him and rested my head on his shoulder. He didn't try to hug back.

It wasn't like that, he said.

He's drunk, Doak. Don't go.

I was young and stupid.

He unclasped my hands and backed away from me.

I reached for his hands. Please stay.

He shook his head. I made a mistake, he said. The kind you can't make right. The kind you just have to live with.

I hugged him and he pressed his lips lightly on my forehead. Then he turned and started for the door. He got halfway and then stopped to pick up one of Ariel's naked Barbies. He looked at the doll and then at me and he smiled.

Take care of those kids, he said. He put the doll on the coffee table.

I will, I said as I watched him walk away.

SOME OF THIS IS TRUE

After all these years I get a call for jury duty. Miami-Dade Felony Court, which is like the major leagues for your criminal element. The case is going to be a no-brainer – Vietnamese babysitter accused of baby-shaking. I look at her sitting at that defendant's table all scary-eyed and I know she didn't mean to hurt that baby. She just wanted to make him stop crying. She hasn't learned yet that everything we want has a price.

To be honest, I'm not too stoked about being called. But after the judge gives us this pep talk about how it's our civic responsibility, I'm like, okay, I'll do my duty. I want to be a good citizen.

The lawyers start asking questions. The defense lawyers don't want anyone who's prejudiced against gooks and the offense lawyers don't want anyone who's too wishy-washy. By the time they call my name they only need one more juror. There are three of us left – me, some Mexican chick with ugly snake tattoos on both forearms, and a creepy guy with BO and a serious dandruff problem. Capital L losers. I'm a lock for that last spot.

I swear to tell the truth, the whole truth, so help me God, and when the prosecutor asks me if my real name is Victoria Ramirez I say no, my real name is Vicki Sanchez. He gives me that look I always get when I tell people my real name. His eyes get all squinty and he says, "The Vicki Sanchez?"

I was born too early. Nowadays I would have made it on to Larry King Live, been interviewed by Perez Hilton and probably had a gig on the Tonight Show. Could have sold my story to the Enquirer for a half mil easy.

My family escaped from Cuba in a boat with everything we owned packed in two lousy suitcases. I never got to finish high school. I had to work so my baby brother, Felipe, could go to college and make something of himself. He's a dermatologist in Palm Beach and doesn't want anything to do with me. Says I shamed the family.

I could have been a great runner, but I had to work for a living. Not like those bony chicks from the suburbs in their fancy running clubs. After it was all over the newspapers made fun of me. Made it sound like I was some spectator on a lark who jumped in that race for the last hundred yards.

That's not how it went down.

I made my move outside Newton, right after Heartbreak Hill, almost five miles from the finish line. It was a great plan. I found this place where the road curved over a narrow bridge – out of sight of most spectators. I put on my hoodie to cover my race number and waited. My timing had to be perfect. Took almost two hours until I saw that cop car with its lights blazing, escorting some skinny African dude at the head of the pack. Close behind him were a bunch of guys trying to keep up and then another couple hundred yards before the next clump of runners. I figured there might be a woman in that clump so I made my move. I hadn't done all that work to finish second.

I started to walk along the shoulder as though I were looking for a better spot to watch the race. Kept my head down, didn't make eye contact with anyone, then eased into a slow jog. Soon as I got around the bend, I whipped off the sweatshirt and started running hard. By the time I crossed the creek I was rocking.

And wouldn't you know it? The first spectator to spot me was a dreamy-looking Latin boy. He clapped his hands and yelled, "Adelante, niña!" And then a few more took up the cheer and it just kept growing, all the way to the finish line. No one had ever cheered for me like that before. It was like a dream. My feet hardly touched the pavement. Yeah, I only ran five miles, but that day, I could have run forever.

I just wanted to win something. For once in my life I wanted to stand on the top of the podium and have people respect me. I was young and foolish and when you're young you don't think about tomorrow. I'm fifty-five now. I made a mistake, but that's in the past. I'm not that person any more.

"The Vicki Sanchez?" the prosecutor asks.

I just stare at him because, what can I say? He looks over at Tattoo Girl and Dandruff Man and his face twists up like he had a bad burrito for lunch. Then he turns to me and says, "Thank you, Ms. Sanchez, you're excused."

DALTON'S GOOD FORTUNE

Dalton Hall was dying. It had taken four hours to unload the circus trucks and now they had to pitch the tents and assemble the booths. His arms and shoulders throbbed as they tugged on the big-top. The other temps were rheumy-eyed, out-of-luck men just like Dalton, but younger, with harder edges, fresher muscles. Dalton's boot-heel hit a rock in the hardpacked turf and he fell to his knees. The men stopped tugging.

"Come on, old man," said the kid next to him, a skinhead with snake tattoos curled around both arms. "We ain't got all fucking night."

Dalton pushed himself to his feet, his breaths ragged, his hands on his knees. The cough returned, wet and mucousy, like he was drowning. His nose dripped. He swiped his face with the sleeve of his army jacket.

The crew chief jumped down from the bed of his pickup where he'd been barking orders. "Shut up, you little Nazi." He walked over to Dalton and pointed at the combat-side insignia on his shoulder. "12th Cav?" he asked.

"2nd Battalion. Back in '68."

"During Tet?"

"Thon La Chu. We got killed all to hell there." Dalton hawked up a glob of phlegm.

"My brother died at Khe Sanh."

Dalton nodded. The ghosts lived forever.

"Go help my palm reader, Zelda. Her old man got busted and she ain't never going to get that booth up on her own."

Dalton squared up, hands on his hips. "A palm reader?" He spit out the words like bad medicine.

"What? That against your religious principles?"

Dalton spit again, shook his head. "I ain't got no goddamn principles."

Zelda was a skinny country girl, a wispy blonde with light eyes and a hillbilly twang. Nothing like the other one. "Sure do 'preciate all your help, Mr. Hall," she said as Dalton finished nailing up her sign promising, "Honest Readings – Guaranteed Results." "You did right fine work."

"You're welcome, miss."

Zelda pulled out a change purse from her apron pocket. She handed Dalton a greasy dollar bill. "Sorry I ain't got more."

Dalton took the bill. "It's okay. Bossman's paying us."

"Let me give you a reading. On the house." Her smile was so pure, Dalton hated to say no.

"No need, ma'am."

Zelda pouted. "You think I'm a fake."

"No ma'am. It's just I've already been done. In Saigon. When I had a future to tell."

"And what did she reckon your future was?"

"Said my lifeline were broke. Said I'd never make it home."

Zelda took his hand. She studied his face while she ran her smooth warm hands over his palm. Her touch felt magical. "You believed her," she said. It wasn't a question.

Dalton tried to pull his hand away, but he couldn't. "Yeah, every goddamn bullshit word."

"And what happened?"

"I'm still here, ain't I?"

"What happened at Thon La Chu?" she asked. Her twang was gone. Her blue eyes seemed to stare through him.

"What? How do you...?"

"Tell me, Dalton."

He took a deep breath and let it out slowly. "NVA had us pinned down on the side of the mountain. We knew come daybreak they'd attack. I figured I'm a dead man, so I picked up my M-16 and headed for the mountaintop. Wanted to be as close to Heaven as I could get."

"And your comrades?"

"Some of them boys followed me, some didn't. Most of us made it to the top. Them boys that stayed behind..." Dalton shook his head.

"I reckon she saved your life," Zelda said, twangy again.

"You're crazy."

She turned over his palm. "Look, here. See this bump under your little finger? You have great moral courage, Dalton Hall."

Dalton stared at his palm. "Me? You are crazy. I ain't no hero."

"You have principles, Dalton, but see this hollow under your thumb?"

Zelda rubbed Dalton's fingertips over the smooth depression.

"That's where you get your physical courage. Recklessness. You're not wild, Dalton. You're a gentle man."

"She said I was going to die."

"She knew that in a world gone mad only the reckless survive."

Dalton bowed his head, cradled his palm. For the first time in forty years he cried. The tears fell into his upturned hand and trickled to the groove etched across his palm. "What's this line?" he asked, pointing to the river of tears.

Zelda brushed her lips against his cheek and whispered in his ear. "That's the heart line, Dalton. You have such a very fine heart."

THE QUICK PICK

I t was two a.m. and The Blade was closed. Anita's daughter was asleep on the cot in the manager's office where Anita had left her when her shift began at nine. Ray and Anita stood on the deck behind Winston, who remained slumped at his corner table, his head resting gentle in the crook of his arm. Winston was dead.

Anita had thought he'd been lulled to sleep by the pounding waves that each day brought the ocean a little closer to the front deck of The Blade. In another twenty years the island would be gone and the aging hippies like Winston and the runaways like Anita and the social misfits like Ray would have to find another home.

Winston's hand still clutched the lottery ticket. After his usual comments about how fine she looked in her red tube top he had bragged to Anita about winning the Quick Pick. "Hit three numbers, Nita. See? That's five grand. Tell Ray I want the good rum tonight." She had brought him three shots, one for each winning number. Doubles.

She poked him in the back. Harder this time. "See, Ray, he's dead. And there's the ticket."

Ray tugged the ticket out of Winston's hand. Ray was in his thirties and had a day job on the mainland as a roofer. Wiry and strong, and with his roofer tan, almost as dark as Anita. His dirty blonde hair was ponytailed and he had a vintage seventies mustache that Anita figured was his attempt to hide bad teeth. It didn't, but he was still one of the better prospects on the island.

Ray held the ticket up in the moonlight and turned it all around. He tugged on his mustache, smiled, and wrapped his arms around Anita. He cupped her ass and pulled her close. "Looks like Winston left you a bodacious tip, babe."

"We split, Ray. Fifty-fifty."

"No, no, no, darlin. You earned that. Two years of that old fart staring at your tits and grabbing your ass."

"I can't cash it."

Ray frowned and rubbed his chin. The lottery office required ID. Anita didn't even have a green card. "What about the paycheck store? They'll do anything for money."

"They take sixty percent. Fifty-fifty, Ray." She took his hand and brought it up to her breast. "Please."

Ray smiled at her. "You're mighty persuasive."

Anita ran her hands up and down Ray's sinewy body. She closed her eyes and listened to the surf as it rolled up the shore with her future. Ray was a thief, but he wasn't a runner. He would be a good father. He would cash the ticket and he would discover it was a four pick that paid fifty grand, not five. He would give her twenty-five hundred dollars and she would never let him know that she knew. He would invite her into his home. And as the ocean crept ever closer he would use the lottery windfall to buy The Blade from its mainland owners and he and Anita would live there and raise her daughter. Together. Until the ocean redeemed them.

THE TOLL COLLECTOR

One day this gal, a waitress I figured, drove up in an old Fairmont. She was pretty in a Polish sort of way. Blonde hair pulled back, deep-set eyes. Solid. Two kids in car-seats in the back – a light-haired girl about two and a chunky baby boy. Her uniform was creased like she just pulled it out of the box. ZADIE according to her nametag. I figured it's her first day on the job because she's all nervous, rooting around in her purse for the toll. Gave me a dollar bill and a big smile. Told me she was sorry, like she'd been keeping me from something important. I handed her two quarters and she said, "Thank you, Patrick."

I nearly fell out of the booth. After that, every day, it's, "Thank you, Patrick." I wanted to say, "You're welcome, Zadie," but that would have been crossing a line. Then just before Christmas the boy's seat was empty. Zadie didn't smile. She just took her change and drove off like everyone else. Didn't see her again until Easter.

She looked tired when she pulled up to the booth. Her uniform hung on her. The little girl sat beside her in the front seat. No car seats. No baby boy. When Zadie handed me her money she smiled, but that was just because she's a nice person. I squeezed her hand and gave her a little nod. I'm not supposed to do that.

NINA'S SONG

W hen Nick Pomeroy was 12 years old he lost his three-year old sister, Nina, at Woodfield Mall. Nick had wanted to stay home and play basketball with his friends, but his mom had insisted he come along to help her with Nina, as his father was unavailable – having conveniently scheduled a Saturday morning meeting with one of his tax clients. It was the week before Christmas and Nick was annoyed with Nina who wouldn't stop singing that stupid song about the wheels on the bus as he pushed her stroller through the hordes of shoppers while his mom checked out the display windows, searching for the right gift for her sister.

After passing a number of acceptable stores, she stopped in front of the Victoria's Secret display, which was occupied by three shapely mannequins wearing Santa's hats and skimpy underwear. "Come on, Nick, I want to check out this store."

Nick could feel his face coloring. "I'm not going in there." The shop was packed with women and high school girls. "There's no room for her stupid stroller."

His mom bit her lip as she stared into the crowded shop. "Okay, you stay here with Nina. Don't let her out of your sight. I'll just be a few minutes."

After his mom disappeared into the store, Nina started to pound her feet on the stroller. She pointed across the way to the mechanical Santa in front of Radio Shack. "Santa, Nicky!"

"We have to stay here," Nick said.

"Santa! Santa! Santa!"

Nick sighed. "Okay." He wheeled over and parked Nina in front of Santa. In the Radio Shack display an employee was playing the videogame DOOM. Nick had never seen such a cool game. The player ran down dark, spooky hallways, shooting bad guys at every turn. Around and around and then, Kablam!

"Look, Nina, big boom." Nick reached for the stroller, but it wasn't there.

He never, of course, forgot that moment. His heart beating so hard it hurt. The cold, sick feeling in his stomach as he ran from store to store, calling Nina's name. And that look on his mom's face when she ran out of the store.

They never found Nina. She vanished from the face of the earth and no one saw her leave. It was Nick's fault. He understood that. The Pomeroys were not emotional people. His parents never yelled at him. Never said they blamed him. Never had to tell him they loved him anyway. Those things were understood.

The Pomeroys were practical people. They didn't cling to false hopes. They waited a year and then one day when Nick came home from school the pictures of Nina were gone from the living room wall and her room had been converted to a spare bedroom that no one ever used. Nick understood. Nina was gone and there was nothing else to do, but go on with their lives.

Nick went on to college at UCLA and fell in love with Donna Clement, a dark-eyed Italian girl who worked in the Student Union. They got married before his second year of law at USC and moved into an attic apartment in the Clement home. The Clements argued and hugged and played loud board games, which often ended with someone throwing something. Nick loved them very much. He never told Donna or her parents that he once had a sister named Nina.

Cassie was born two years after Nick graduated from USC Law. His parents wanted to come out and see her, but Nick put them off. Too hectic, with a new baby and the long hours at the law firm. His parents understood. They were practical people.

Donna's gift for his 30th birthday was three airline tickets to Chicago. Nick looked at the tickets and shook his head. "It's not a good time. Work..."

"Stop it, Nick. I haven't seen your parents since the wedding. And Cassie needs to meet her other grandparents. No discussion, Mister." She kissed him and Nick decided maybe it was time.

His parents had aged well. His father had retired early and, unbelievably, taken up gardening. Their front lawn, which had always been as antiseptically groomed and edged as a golf course, was now speckled with outbursts of mums and daisies and wildflowers. His mother, even more surprising, had acquired a piano and taken lessons. They were very happy to meet Cassie, and spoiled her even more than her other grandparents.

On the third day of their visit, his mom brought out Nick's toy box, which was filled with his old Ninja turtle paraphernalia. She dressed Cassie in his Donatello costume. As she rolled up the pants and sleeves, Nick's heart twinged as he remembered doing that same thing for Nina. Cassie padded over to the toy box and discovered his Ninja trifold wallet. She pulled out a photo that had been pasted on red construction paper and framed with popsicle sticks.

"Who's this, Nana?" She ran over to her grandmother. Nick watched as his mother studied the photo. Her chin trembled ever so slightly.

"That's my little sister, Nina," Nick said. "She was the same age as you, honey."

Donna looked up from her magazine. "Your sister?"

"Where is she, Daddy? Can I play with her?"

30

Nick's throat tightened. "I lost her. I was supposed to keep her safe and I..." The words choked him. He just stood in the middle of their living room aware of Cassie and his mother and Donna all staring at him. Waiting. "I lost her and—"

"No, Nicky," his mom said softly. She walked over and hugged him. "It wasn't your fault."

She took Cassie by the hand and led her over to the piano. "Come here, darling. I want to teach you a song that my Nina used to love."

KID PARKER GETS A TITLE FIGHT AT THE GARDEN
WORLD WELTERWEIGHT CHAMPIONSHIP
KID PARKER VS. JOHNNY SAXTON

June 22, 1954 – Madison Square Garden

O kay we're back now. Monty Gerard broadcasting from ringside at Madison Square Garden – fifth round of this scheduled twelve-rounder. At stake, the Welterweight Championship of the World. Well, not really. Johnny Saxton has used the inexperienced Kid Parker as a punching bag for four rounds. Only question that remains is how much more punishment can The Kid take?

There's the bell. Saxton's out of the corner fast. Kid's flatfooted – no bounce. Shuffles to the center of the ring. Right eye's swolled shut. Left eye not much better. Saxton a left to the Kid's chin – another – and another. Right to the body. That one hurt. Parker ties him up. They break. Parker misses with a wild roundhouse. Saxton moves inside. Punishing body shot. Now a left to the head, right to the jaw, another to the body. Parker tries to tie him up. Saxton pushes him off. Another left to the chin, right to the body. Whoa – the Kid's down...

Julie turned off the radio. Even in the boxers' dressing room she could hear the roar from the crowd when he went down. Lloyd was right – he wasn't ready for a title fight. Johnny Saxton was a beast, and Lloyd, well Lloyd really was a kid. A sweet kid, but what a schnook. He was happy ham-and-egging at the K-of-C for chump change and trinkets. Nobody turns down a title fight at the Garden. Take the fight, she said. Be a man. Make some real bread.

Julie sighed, then stubbed out her cigarette, pushed open the dressing room door and headed up the ramp. When she got to ringside, Lloyd was standing wobbly-legged in the center of the ring. The referee stepped aside and motioned to Johnny Saxton who bounced menacingly in his neutral corner. Arnie Levin, Lloyd's useless manager, knocked a chunk of ash from his fat cigar into the spit-bucket and stared out at the action like he was just another spectator.

"Stop the goddamn fight, Arnie," Julie screamed from the aisle.

32

Arnie looked over his shoulder at her and his face got all scrunched up like he was working on a fart. A pimply kid in an oversized usher uniform tapped Julie on the shoulder. "You can't stand there, Ma'am."

"Listen, Zit-face, that's my husband up there getting his ass kicked. I'll stand wherever I goddamn please."

Arnie Levin was in trouble. He'd bet five Gs with Joey Giradello that The Kid would last five rounds. Signed over the Kid's purse to make the bet. The Kid had heart and Johnny Saxton was a lazy guinea who didn't usually wake up till the tenth round. But Johnny must have some pussy waiting for him tonight because he'd woke up early and was acting like a mad dog with a rag doll. The Kid looked like he was searching for a soft place to land. And now that bitch Julie had to show up. Arnie would rather stiff Joey G. than tell Julie Parker he'd just pissed away her husband's purse.

Arnie banged his diamond pinkie-ring on the side of the bucket. "Hey, Kid!" From the panicked-look in Lloyd's left eye, Arnie could tell he was ready to go down. Arnie flicked his head toward the aisle. "Julie says you better not quit."

I got hold of Johnny Saxton like we're in love. Dago's too goddamn tough. I gotta go down. Now what, Arnie? Ten goddamn fights he never says jack. Now he's going to get instructional? Shit. Julie's here. She's pissed. Jesus fucking Mary and Joseph, how long till the bell?

Come on Ref, don't break us up, yet. Can't breathe. Can't see. Backpedal. Find some air. Johnny won't give me any space. Gotta protect the chin. Ahh, but he's pounding my gut. Stop it man. Stop it. I gotta bring the gloves down. Just for a...

The reporter from ESPN is doing a piece on the Bloodiest Fights of the Century. She hands Tommy Quinn a yellowed newspaper. He doesn't have to look at it. It's the front page of the New York Daily News for June 23, 1954. The two-inch high headline screams, "MURDER AT THE GARDEN," and below the headline the picture of referee Tommy Quinn standing over a comatose Kid Parker.

"This fight doesn't qualify," Tommy says.

"I'm sorry." The reporter wrinkles up her freckled nose. She's blonde, pretty. Used to be an Olympic swimmer or skier. Great rack, dumb as a box of rocks.

"Wasn't a bloody fight. The Kid wasn't a bleeder. If he'd been a bleeder I'd have stopped the fight."

"Have you ever read the coroner's report?" she asks, her eyes bugged out, like Tommy has just tried to cop a feel. She turns and looks directly into the camera. Starts reading from the report. Lots of medical bullshit that basically said The Kid's liver had been pounded into jelly and his brain into oatmeal. Tommy didn't need any goddamn coroner to tell him that. Johnny Saxton had pulverized The Kid's guts and when The Kid dropped his guard Johnny practically took off his head with a straight right hand. Tommy figured The Kid was dead before he hit the canvas. For sure he was gone before Tommy finished counting him out.

"...you were the referee, Mr. Quinn. Wasn't it up to you to stop the fight?"

"Nope." Tommy crushes out his cigarette and pulls out his pack of Camels. "Want one?"

She gives him that look again. "Why didn't you stop it?"

Tommy shakes his head. These kids today, they just don't get it. He lights his cigarette and blows the smoke toward the ceiling. "It was a Title Fight."

PICKUP LINE AT THE RITZ CARLTON

T hirty-one years is a long time. You must be a good husband.
Not really. Do you want another daiquiri?
Absolutely. So what's kept you together?

My wife saves college class notes, twenty-year old cancelled checks, empty margarine tubs...

So?

She doesn't throw anything away.

LAST CALL

Two hours into their Newark to London flight, their plane was struck by lightning. They had been flying at 39,000 feet – miles above the storm that pounded the north Atlantic. Frank had settled back into his comfy first-class seat to savor his third glass of chardonnay. He was enjoying the lightshow on display far below when two lightning bolts fused into a ferocious burst that mushroomed up from the storm clouds and enveloped their plane. For an instant their world was nuclear-blast bright. Frank squeezed his eyes shut. The blazing image of his wine glass was seared on the backs of his eyelids. And then the cabin went dark and unnaturally quiet. Frank's tongue tingled and the wine, which he reflexively sipped, had a bitter, metallic taste.

Toby, the fair-haired McKinsey consultant Frank had been assigned to shepherd to the London office, had been clicking away on his laptop almost from the moment they left Newark. When he had powered up his computer Frank had noticed, somewhat to his surprise, that Toby's screensaver had displayed a photo of Toby on a beach in Hawaii with his arms draped around a pretty black woman and a smiling, copper-colored boy.

The laptop had gone blank. Toby, his hands still stuck on the keyboard, stared at Frank with unblinking eyes. "What happened?"

Whimpers and cries could be heard in the economy section, but first class remained eerily quiet, as though those privileged travelers were on another plane. A throaty whirr rumbled through the plane like a generator starting and then the auxiliary lights in the cabin came back on. "I don't know," Frank said, staring out into the darkness. "Some kind of electrical discharge."

A flight attendant emerged from the cockpit, her face not as stoic as it should have been. She huddled with the other attendants, then they fanned out down the aisles telling everyone to stay in their seats and remain calm.

"Why is it so quiet, Frank?"

Frank had been an engineer for thirty years. He'd survived TQM from Bain and Best-practices from BCG and Matrix-management from Booz and he had planned on surviving whatever bullshit concept Toby and the McKinsey prima donnas came up with, but right now it didn't look so good. "Both engines have been knocked out," he said.

"But they must have a backup engine or something, right?" Toby asked.

Frank almost smiled. "I don't think so. Some consultant probably told them they'd only need it for one out of a thousand flights. Not a good value proposition."

"Seriously, Frank. What's their plan?"

Frank put a finger to his lips. The crew had enough problems trying to figure out how to restart those engines without them creating a panic. "The RAM auxiliary turbine in the back of the plane will give the crew hydraulics and navigational capabilities, but it can't power the plane," he whispered. "Right now we're a hundred ton glider. The crew need to get those engines restarted. They can keep us from stalling by angling the plane downward."

"It doesn't feel like we're losing altitude," Tony said.

"Two thousand feet per minute."

Toby looked up at the ceiling as he did the arithmetic. "Nineteen minutes?"

"Give or take."

The awful quiet was shattered by the high-pitched screech of the starboard engine – metal on metal and then it stopped and they tried the port engine. More screeching, but that engine didn't start either.

Toby sighed, closed his eyes, and sat back in his seat. Quietly he murmured the 23rd psalm. Then he grabbed the briefcase at his feet and retrieved his Blackberry.

If Frank and Marcie had had children, he could have had a son about Toby's age now. A kid might have made a difference in their lives. Maybe Frank would have been a better father than he was a husband. He reached over and put his hand on Toby's forearm. "We're a thousand miles from land, son. There's no cell service."

"You gotta have faith, Frank." Toby punched a number and pressed the phone to his ear. His forehead was a grid of concentration as though he could will the phone call to go through. "Hey Sonya, it's me... can you hear me? ... You're breaking up... Listen, babe. Pray for us.... Me and Frank and everyone on this plane... okay? Kiss Robert for me. I love you... Sonya... can you hear me?... Hello?..." He looked at the phone screen and then dropped the phone back in his briefcase.

The plane had descended into the teeth of the storm and turbulence rocked the aircraft. The pilot banked hard left and then right and increased the angle of descent to avoid stalling. Now everyone could tell they were going down and wails and prayers and scrotum-shriveling screams filled the cabin.

"I can't believe you got through," Frank said. He tried to imagine calling Marcie. What would he say? That he was sorry? That in the last minute of his life he was thinking about her? Would that be a comfort?

"Do you want to pray with me, Frank?" Toby asked.

Frank looked at his watch. They'd been descending for fifteen minutes. Soon they would emerge from the storm cloud to face the angry Atlantic. They would hit the water at 200 knots and that would tear the plane apart. Anyone who survived wouldn't last long in the frigid water. "It's too late for me." He squeezed Toby's hand and turned back to his window – watching as though he were just a spectator.

The plane burst out of the clouds. The ocean loomed in all directions. They were close enough so Frank could see whitecaps and ridges of waves. And then to his total bafflement on the horizon was an airport beacon. It had to be the St. John's airport on the east coast of Newfoundland. Or Atlantis.

It would take a miracle.

He reached for Toby's hand. "On second thought..."

TWO ROADS DIVERGED IN A YELLOW WOOD

P rairie Lane was lined with new houses, all identical, like the plastic pieces in Wanda's Monopoly game. The Midwest summer sun had turned the subdivision's freshly-sodded lawns brown and brittle. Wanda's father, as usual, had been way too optimistic. He was confident the new neighborhood would be clamoring for the Compton Pictured Encyclopedia. They were not. So far only one resident had taken her brochure. And he had been certain she could make it to the end of Prairie Lane by noon – he planned to pick her up so she could brief him on all the great prospects – but it was already eleven and she was nowhere near the end of the road.

Wanda's short frizzy hair had clumped with sweat and her stubby arms ached as she lugged the briefcase of sample books and brochures toward the next house. There was a kiddie-pool in the front yard and it reminded her that her older brother Zachary was lifeguarding at the community center while his girlfriend Kelly sunned herself by his lifeguard chair. Kelly, with her silky blonde hair and her perfect teeth and those cute little dimples, would be dribbling on the Coppertone and spreading it down her flat belly and between her smooth thighs and...

Wanda needed a glass of water. She knocked on the door of 87 Prairie Lane. There was a muffled voice from the kitchen which sounded like, "Go away." But Wanda would not go away. She needed that glass of water. She knocked again.

A frustrated moan and then footsteps and the door opened. Standing in front of her was a boy from school. Ricky something. He was a senior, a year behind her brother. A quiet boy, not many friends. He had one of those cheap Bic pens clutched in his fist and his usually slicked-down hair was messed. His eyes were red. "What do you want?" he asked.

"Hello, Ricky. My name's Wanda Russell." She stepped quickly past him into the house as her father had taught her. "I'd like to introduce you to—"

"Not interested."

Wanda smiled and set her briefcase on the linoleum. She flipped open the clasps and pulled out the sample book. "Did you realize, Ricky, that for just one dollar a week your family can possess the world's finest encyclopedia." She handed the open book to Ricky.

"It's Richard, not Ricky." He glanced at the volume. "This book thinks Eisenhower's still president."

"Well let me assure you, Richard, that when the annual update arrives in the mail this fall, it will have a comprehensive report on the election of President Kennedy."

"Listen, Wendy—"

"Wanda."

"—I don't want your goddamn second-rate encyclopedia. We've got the World Book." He pointed his pen at the row of green and beige volumes in the built-in bookcase.

"I see. Well then, could I please have a glass of water?" Wanda took the book back from him.

Richard looked to the ceiling and muttered something to himself. "Wait here," he said through clenched teeth. He pushed open the swinging door to the kitchen. Before the door swung shut, Wanda saw that the floor was littered with crumbled sheets of paper. There was a note pad on the kitchen table and next to the pad, like a table setting, was a big revolver. When Richard reemerged with the glass of water the gun was gone.

"Here." He handed her the glass.

Wanda's heart pounded. She stood in the doorway and gulped the tepid water. She stared at Richard as she drank, but he wouldn't meet her gaze. She had to take action. "Let me show you something you won't find in that old World Book." She walked into the living room and sat down on the sofa. "Come here, Richard."

"You need to go," he said. He looked at the kitchen door and then at Wanda and his eyes bugged, like he was holding his breath. Wanda smiled and patted the seat next to her. Richard exhaled a long sigh, then walked over and sat down. His foot started tapping.

"Do you like poetry?" Wanda opened the sample book to the bookmarked section. "My father used to read Robert Frost to me every night before I went to bed. This was my favorite." She flipped through the pages trying to decide quickly which of those awful poems she would deem her favorite. Not Death of the Hired Man or Home Burial. She turned the page. Stopping by Woods on a Snowy Evening. Perfect. Short and it even rhymed. She started to read. Richard stopped fidgeting halfway through the poem. And when she got to the final, Miles to go before I sleep, a tear rolled down his cheek.

Wanda closed the book and hugged it to her chest. "My father loved that poem. He said he would read it whenever he had a bad day. It made him realize life had all these great possibilities and even if he hadn't sold a goldarn thing all day, things would be better tomorrow."

Richard wrinkled up his face. "That doesn't make any sense. That's not what the poem's saying."

40

"Well, what do you think it means, Mister Know-It-All." She handed him the book.

He studied the page and then looked up at her, with the hint of a smile. "It means he has a lot of things to do and doesn't have time to waste buying a stupid out-of-date encyclopedia."

Wanda took the book back from him. "They don't like me that much at school, either."

"What are you talking about?" he asked.

"My father told me I didn't have to be like everyone else. He said I won't have to live here my whole life. He'd always say…" She tucked her chin and lowered her voice. "'There's a whole goldarn world out there, Wanda – lots of different kinds of folks. So don't fret, darling, cause you'll find your way.'"

Richard smiled again. "He really said goldarn?"

"Yeah. He's funny that way."

"Your father sounds like a real pain-in-the-ass."

Wanda shrugged her shoulders. "I know." She stood up and handed the book to Richard. "Here. Take this. It's a two dollar value, but I'll let you have it for a dollar. Don't pay me now. I'll be back next week to collect." She held out her hand. "Deal?"

Richard sighed again. "Okay," he said.

They shook hands and Wanda stepped out of the house into the bright mid-morning sunshine. She stared down Prairie Lane. She had miles to go.

THE SUMMER OF '66

If you were headed to some fancy college like twin-sister Lucy, you might've called spotting Joe Rizzi hitchhiking out front of the Carvel Soft Ice Cream stand serendipity. But college doesn't want you, so you're going to Nam. So is Joe.

You drive a tomato-red 1960 Ford Sunliner convertible – a 4-barrel 300 horsepower gas hog. The dual-exhaust glasspacks rattle and clank as you pull to the curb. "Need a ride, Joe?"

"What the fuck you think?" he says, as he folds himself into the seat like a muscle-bound cobra. He tosses his gym bag into the backseat. A pack of Lucky's is squeezed into the sleeve of his white tee. "Smoke?" He mouths one from the pack.

You have a rule. No smoking in the Sunliner. Lucy says that's stupid. "It's a convertible, Jimmy." Last week, when you let her borrow the car for the fancy graduation party at her fancy boyfriend's house, you made her promise. But Joe's not asking permission, just offering a smoke.

"No thanks," you say.

You cruise past the drive-in, which is still showing cool Steve McQueen in "The Sand Pebbles." Before you ship out you plan to take Jane Macri, but you're waiting for a better makeout-movie. The drive-in will close in the fall of '76. Their last picture, "One Flew Over the Cuckoo's Nest," is also not a good makeout-movie. By then you won't care.

"I need gas. You got a buck?"

Joe leans into the backseat to grab his wallet from his gym bag. "Hey Jimmy, who'd you fuck with this balloon?"

A green rubber dangles from his fingers.

Goddamn Lucy.

The Sunliner fishtails, then skids into the path of a Genesee Beer truck.

Your car is crushed, but somehow Joe survives. He'll die two years later. An ambush at Hoc Mon. The Legion Post will honor him with a park bench.

THE BIRDHOUSE BUILDER

W e're in the seasonal interregnum. The last winter snow hangs on in the shadows of my parents' two-story colonial, while the first wave of migratory birds circle the neighborhood, checking out the accommodations. Dad wants to reconstruct the birdhouse. The son of a farmer, he can fix broken things. Build stuff. Use tools the right way. I have none of those skills. As a boy I was his unhappy assistant. "Hand me the needlenose," he would say, his arm reaching back, head buried in the bowels of the cranky Maytag washing machine. I would stare at the battlefield of tools surrounding him and try to pick one that resembled a needle nose. I usually guessed wrong.

He has disassembled the remnants of the old birdhouse. Measured the wood slats and created a spec sheet. He doesn't trust his memory anymore. It's less reliable than that little boy who would hand him vise grips instead of pliers. When I was a kid these projects would start with a trip to Ike's Hardware. That was in the small town where I grew up, not this resort town where my parents have grown old. Back then Dad never had a spec sheet – usually just a scrap of paper with a few odd numbers on it. Ike's was full of open bins of screws and bolts and nails and rolls of sandpaper and shelf after shelf of hand tools. It had a metallic, oily smell – different from a Home Depot or Loews or one of those garden-hardware-lumber behemoths.

That's where we go now. Krendall's Home Center. It has patio furniture out front. And a greeter. My dad walks slowly, dragging his left leg. He had a hip replaced ten years ago. The greeter asks me if she can help us. My dad says, "Specialty Lumber." She smiles at him and tells me to go see Ray in the lumberyard behind the store.

Ray looks just like Ike – sandy crewcut and a red hardware apron. But now he's twenty years younger than me. Dad would usually tell Ike what he was working on and Ike would nod and maybe rub his chin and then hustle off to retrieve the hardware. Dad tries to describe the birdhouse to Ray, but Ray can't follow him. I can't either. There is a thin bead of sweat on his upper lip and I want him to wipe it away, but he just starts over, trying to explain his project. Ray turns away from him and asks me what it is we want.

I'm just the boy. Why is he asking me?

"Show him the paper, Dad." He has forgotten about his sheet. Dad pats his pockets and on his fourth pocket he finds it. Ray looks at Dad's detailed drawing and the list of pieces and parts and then he nods like Ike.

We bring home a sack of wood slats and black enamel and half-inch wood screws. Dad lays everything out on his work table. He picks up one of the slats and turns it all around. His hands shake and his grip on the piece is tentative as though he doesn't know what to do with it. My mom calls from the kitchen. Lunch is ready. After lunch Dad takes a nap.

Three years later, after my dad dies and I move Mom to the assisted living facility, I clean out their house. I find the birdhouse parts stuffed back in their Krendall Home Center bag tucked away in a far corner of the garage.

TIME DON'T RUN OUT ON ME

T ina would have preferred a quiet Friday night alone at home, but she had promised her friend Annie that she would go out with her. Annie, young, with energy to burn, had spent her day in the air-conditioned comfort of the Caterpillar assembly plant, while Tina, Maple Spring's only postal carrier, had labored eight hours in the hot-towel Missouri heat, lugging Victoria Secret and Bass Pro Sports catalogs to every household in town. And this was Tina's weekend to be on call – she was an EMT with the Maple Springs Volunteer Fire Department – so she wasn't going to be much more than Annie's designated driver.

Annie had dropped her two kids with her mother and now paced anxiously in front of her mom's house. She was wearing red satin shorts and a wifebeater that was stretched tight across the boobs she'd acquired two weeks after her cheating, soon-to-be-ex-husband had shipped out to Iraq. Tina pulled up to the curb and Annie jumped in.

"You in a hurry?" Tina asked. "Or is your mom's a/c not working again?"

Annie had pulled down the car visor and was checking her makeup in the mirror. "First she starts on my hair. Says platinum looks cheap. Then for the millionth freaking time she tells me I shouldn't have spent Granny's inheritance on a boob job. And when she's got that all out of her system she says I look like a Hooter's waitress. So I decided to wait outside."

"You don't look like a Hooter's waitress..."

"Thank you."

"...more like a pornstar."

Annie continued to touch up her lipstick while she gave Tina the finger. She finished and slammed the visor up. "And you look like the farmer's daughter."

Tina had on her short-short jeans cutoffs and a white blouse tied in front, that showed off her flat stomach. She was twenty years older than Annie, but had a trim body and a smooth unlined face, so most guys didn't notice a huge age difference. Of course when Annie dressed like Jenna Jameson most guys didn't notice Tina at all. "Where should we go?" she asked.

"How about Jake's?" Annie said.

Jake's was a biker–hillbilly bar. Mostly locals. It wasn't Tina's favorite place, but she didn't say anything, just maybe raised her eyebrows a bit.

"Hey. It's a fun place," Annie said. "A family bar."

45

"Yeah if your old man's in the joint, or your mom's turning tricks, it's a great place for the family."

"Well then it's a perfect place for you because all you do is make fun of people. You don't ever give any of these guys a chance," Annie said. "And don't give me that look like you're my mother."

"Your problem, Annie, is you give everyone a chance. You fall for a line from some guy just because he ignored you in high school. You can do better. Don't settle for those losers," she said.

"What about you? Don't you ever want to meet someone? You like being alone?" Annie asked.

Tina didn't want to be alone, but she'd waited too long – all the good candidates had been taken years ago. She ignored Annie and concentrated on her driving. Main Street had turned into Highway 60 and was crowded with folks escaping town for the weekend. Jake's was two miles east of town, back in the hills.

Annie put her hand on Tina's shoulder, but Tina shook it off. "I'm sorry, Tina. Don't be mad."

"There are worse things than being alone," Tina whispered.

"I know," Annie said. She turned away and stared out her window.

Jake's parking lot was riddled with potholes and tire ruts. The front section was packed with Harleys and pickups so Tina steered her little Camry around the potholes and headed to the back.

"Where you going?" Annie asked.

Tina gave her a look. "I think the family parking's in the rear."

They both laughed and the great loneliness debate was tabled for at least awhile.

As the bouncer checked their IDs, Tina reminded Annie that she was on call and Annie might have to get her own ride home.

"No problem," Annie said. "I'm very resourceful." She laughed.

"Try a taxi. They're cheaper," Tina said.

"That's no fun."

All the tables were filled, but they found two seats at the bar. They had barely sat down before the pretty boy sitting next to Annie offered to buy them both a drink. Tina had to stay sober, but Annie drank enough for both of them. Two margaritas, then out to the dance floor with pretty boy. Tina was glad to see them go. The boy had bragged nonstop about his real estate deals. He was quite impressed with himself.

The wall behind the bar was mirrored so the bar patrons didn't have to turn around to check out who might be arriving. The man seated to her left caught Tina's eye in the mirror. "I see your friend's left you for that smooth-talking cowboy."

She smiled back at him. "He's a real estate mogul. Said he's going to buy the armory out on Highway 50, turn it into condos. And he's got a nice ass."

"Don't know about the ass, but he sure as hell ain't no Donald Trump."

"No?"

"Nah. I can tell by his hands. If you hadn't spent so much time looking at his ass, you'd have seen it."

She laughed and turned to look at him directly. "Ass-studying is serious work," she said.

He held out his hand, "Name's Clayton?"

Tina's heart skipped. "Clayton? Clayton Stonemason? Oh my god. It is you. Tina Bennett. Remember me?" She shook his hand. The man was coiled on the barstool, not planted like a regular. He was lean, with wheat-colored hair and a grooved, handsome face. She could see in this man the boy she had once known, decades ago.

Clayton embraced Tina's hand with both of his hands. "You look great, Tina." He had tilted his head and was staring at her as though he was looking for this girl who claimed she knew him.

"Do you really remember me?" she asked. He had been four years ahead of her in school. Tina had only been fifteen, but was dragged along by her older sister to the draft lottery party Clayton's girlfriend had organized in the vacant lot next to the Burlington Northern tracks. All the draft-eligible boys and their friends had shown up. They had parked their cars in a circle and built a huge bonfire. As the radio announcer called out the dates and draft numbers the boys had listened for the number that would change the course of their life. They drank to the winners and the losers, and the boys with the high numbers had tried not to look relieved, while the boys with the low numbers had tried not to look scared.

Clayton smiled, but he looked sad. "Of course I remember. I kissed you on the hood of my car, then had a big fight with Candy."

"Oh my god. I forgot your girlfriend's name was Candy. Whatever happened to her?"

Clayton laughed. "She forgave me and we got married a year later. I should have kissed you twice."

Tina glanced at Clayton's hands. No ring. Not that that meant anything. Especially at Jakes. "Didn't last?" It wasn't really a question.

He shook his head. "I thought you moved away?"

"Came back five years ago, when my mom got sick. So tell me about the hands, Clayton."

Clayton took out his cigarettes and tapped the pack on the bar. "A person's hands tell a story. More than most folks realize." He lit his cigarette and took a deep drag and then blew the smoke toward the ceiling. "I noticed that guy when I came in. Not bad-looking, jeans pressed nice, button-down shirt, hair all moussed."

"I thought we were talking about his hands?"

"I'm getting to it. You in a hurry?"

"Sorry. Didn't mean to rush the hand wizard."

"Okay. He's talking to Blondie..."

"Annie."

"...she's looking very hot in that tube top and gym shorts. I figure she probably works at the Caterpillar plant over in Rolla."

Tina punched him in the shoulder. "Damn. You are good. Figure that out from her hands?"

Clayton laughed. "Nobody's looking at that girl's hands. I've seen her in here before with a bunch of other gals from the plant. Anyway...," he looked around and then leaned closer to Tina, "...I hear him telling her about his big real estate plans, but I notice his palms are scrubbed so raw they're pink, but there's oil under his nails. Mechanic fingernails – you can't get that oil out with scrubbing."

Tina turned her hands palms up on the bar. "Read my hands, Clayton."

He took hold of her wrists and brought her hands up close to his face. Then he released them and closed his eyes.

"Are you having a vision?" she asked, tugging on his sleeve.

He clasped her hands again and looked into her eyes. "You work outside, but not a farm. Delivery driver maybe."

"Not bad. I'm a mail carrier. Why are you frowning?"

"There's something more here. You like to help people. Something more than just delivering the mail."

Tina sat back on her stool. "That's right. I'm an EMT for the fire department. Just started last year."

Clayton signaled the bartender for another beer. "Do you want one?" he asked.

"Just tonic water and lime for me. Come on Wizard, you're on a roll. Tell me more."

Clayton pulled back from Tina, like he was trying to bring her in to focus. "Are you sure?"

Tina nodded. "Give me your best shot."

He looked Tina up and down, then took a deep breath and exhaled slowly. "You've never been married. Thought about it when you were younger, plenty of chances, maybe one or two that you thought might be Mr. Right, but you weren't ready. And then later when you were ready, none of the guys seemed good enough.

48

Now you're alone, but you're not lonely. Not too lonely, anyway, but still looking for something."

That was her life. All summed up in one hundred lousy words. "How do you know that?" Tina asked. There was a catch in her voice.

He squeezed her hand. His face was etched with regret. "It's just a barroom trick, Tina. Everybody here's looking for something. Don't let my stupid bullshit get to you."

She sighed and slipped her thumb through the belt loop in the back of his pants. She leaned into him and rested her head on his shoulder. "What about you, Clayton? Did you remarry?"

"Pffft. I'm no good at marriage. Struck out three times."

He looked like she felt. They'd gone in opposite directions and ended up in the same place.

"It's not baseball," she said. "You can take more than three swings."

"You're right," he said. "Baseball's better."

Tina reached over and patted his hand. "Don't worry I wasn't going to ask you to marry me. Not on our first date."

Clayton laughed and then Dusty Springfield started singing You Don't Have to Say You Love Me. "Do you want to dance?" he asked.

"I'd love to." Tina jumped down from her barstool, but then she stopped and grabbed her pager. She didn't want to look at it, but she did. "Dammit. I've gotta go," she said. "EMT call."

Clayton nodded. He was as disappointed as she was. That was a good sign.

"Will you call me?" she asked.

He didn't answer. Instead he leaned over and kissed her softly on the lips. She put her hand on the back of his neck. She didn't want the kiss to end. She didn't want to stand there not hearing him ask for her number.

The pager beeped. "You better run now," he said.

She left him standing at the bar, staring down at his shoes, and hustled out to the parking lot. If she could have stayed, she might have changed his mind. But that was the story of her life – really rotten timing. Why did men have to make everything so complicated? So what if he'd had three lousy marriages. Why not give her a chance? What would he have to lose, besides loneliness?

She started her car and then called Clarence Dobbs, the retired school teacher who acted as the dispatcher for the EMTs and firemen. He picked up immediately.

"Hey Tina, we got a barnburner going tonight. I just sent Pepe and Chuck over to West High Street, a rollover. Need for you and Dennis to go to the United Methodist, somebody passed out. Dennis is already on his way."

"But we're not supposed to make calls on our own," she said. Dennis Williams and Tina were still classified as Trainees. Dennis was an accountant. He had started a month before Tina so he had seniority, but Tina thought he was way too cautious to be an effective EMT. The man couldn't make a decision to save his own life.

"No choice, Tina," Clarence said. "It's a minor call, you guys will do fine. Ten-four."

He hung up before she could ask him for the church address. It probably never occurred to Clarence that Tina might not know the address of every church in town. Methodists. That wasn't one of those storefront churches. It had to be on the west side on Summit or Ferguson where all the mainstream churches were clustered.

Tina raced down Burnham Hill Road, thirty, forty, fifty miles an hour. A quarter mile ahead was the junction with Route 60. As she neared the intersection she took her foot off the gas and the tires on the Camry squealed as she made the hard right turn. The traffic lanes heading into town were uncongested, but the sun hung just above the hills making it difficult to see. Tina squinted and hunched down in the seat, her hands gripped tightly on the steering wheel. At the outskirts of the village she slowed to thirty.

She turned left on Ferguson and two blocks down she could see a stately church bell tower. She pulled into the driveway, but the glass case signboard said, "Welcome to First Pentecostal." She pounded the steering wheel. Her hands ached from gripping the wheel and her mouth was dry. She should have called Clarence back.

She turned back on to Main Street and took a left on Summit. It seemed like the whole street was nothing but churches. Presbyterians and Lutherans at the corner, then the Trinity Baptists in a white-framed mansion. Down from them was a red sandstone building with one bell tower. The sign out front indicated it was the home of the Maple Springs Assembly of God. Across the street another tired Victorian mansion, this one belonged to the First General Baptists. First General didn't look like they were doing as well as their Trinity brethren.

The church next to First General looked like an oasis in the desert. The lawns were lush and well-tended and flowers lined the sidewalk. Tina stopped her car and stared at the welcome board on the side of the church:

United Methodist Church
The Reverend Tommy Blaine
Sunday sermon: "Tend my Lambs, Feed My Sheep"

Tommy Blaine. He was that do-gooder preacher that seemed to get his picture in the local paper every week. She pulled into the driveway, which led to the parking lot in the back of the church. Next to the church in the handicap parking spot was Dennis Williams' Buick Park Avenue. Tina grabbed her gear and ran through the back door, down a long corridor. She found Dennis talking to the preacher, who looked younger in person than in the newspaper photos.

The two men were huddled around a heavyset man who was sitting in a chair with his white shirt unbuttoned and his tie draped around his neck. The man's belly oozed out of the bottom of his undershirt. His face was gray. A trim woman with dark hair was holding his hand. She looked frightened.

Dennis had wrapped up the blood-pressure cuff and was putting it back in his bag. He spotted Tina coming down the hall and gave her his smile, which always looked to Tina like a frown.

"I think we got it under control, Tina. BP's a little elevated, but looks like it was just a panic attack. Jim's daughter's getting married tomorrow."

Dennis was his usual subdued self. Someday Tina wanted to hook him up to the EKG and see if he actually had a heartbeat.

Tina knelt beside the man. "How do you do, sir? My name's Tina Bennett. How are you feeling?" She put her hand on his forearm. His skin had a slippery, slimy feel, sort of like baloney that's been left out on the counter too long.

"This is James Caldwell," Dennis said. "He has a very large car dealership south of town."

Caldwell was a big man. Barrel-chested and at least fifty pounds overweight. He sat up in his chair and smiled at Tina as though he were going to sell her a new car. "I'm okay now, Tina. Feel like a goddamn fool. Started to walk down the aisle and plum fainted." He started buttoning his shirt. "You'd think I was getting married," he said.

The Reverend put his hand on Caldwell's shoulder. "Totally understandable, James. Not every day you give away a daughter."

When the Reverend touched him, Caldwell's smile disappeared and his eyes narrowed as though he were in pain. Tina tried to catch Dennis's eye, but he seemed intent on packing up his bag. James Caldwell did not look like he'd simply had a panic attack.

"Shouldn't we take him over to West Plains?" Tina asked Dennis. The closest hospital, Lutheran General was in West Plains, nineteen miles south of Maple Springs. Caldwell needed to have a complete EKG and cardio work-up, as a precaution. Dennis should have ordered an ambulance.

"No need for that, Tina. I'm okay now," Caldwell said. He stood up and finished buttoning his shirt. The fabric stretched tight across his belly. He turned on his smile, like a man who was used to summoning a smile on demand, but there was no salesman's twinkle in his eyes.

The walkie-talkie Dennis had strapped to his belt squawked. Clarence Dobbs wanted to know the call status. Dennis clicked his radio and spoke quietly into the mouthpiece. "Everything's copasetic, Clarence. False alarm. Ten-four."

"Dennis?" Tina said, her voice tight. Something did not add up.

"What?" Dennis said.

"We need to get him to Lutheran General."

"He's okay, Tina. We don't need to inconvenience everyone."

Tina turned to the woman. "I'm sorry, I didn't catch your name."

"Paula. Paula Caldwell." Her eyes darted from Tina to Dennis and then back to Tina.

"I would strongly recommend that we take your husband over to Lutheran General so he can have an EKG. Just as a precaution."

"But Dennis said—"

"No. She's right," Dennis had set his bag back down, as though it were too heavy for him to carry. "I think it's just a panic attack, but better to be safe than sorry. Let's get him over there so he can get checked out."

Paula Caldwell turned to her husband. Caldwell had walked down the corridor to the hall mirror and was trying to re-tie his tie. "Jim, the rehearsal can wait. We need to get to the hospital."

The tie had come out all wrong. The tail was way too long. He turned to Paula with a look that seemed to say I'm okay, don't make me go. Then the Reverend jumped in with his two cents.

"She's right, James. We don't want to take any chances, do we?" His voice had a sing-songy cadence as though he were talking to a little kid.

Caldwell jerked the tie off and started again. "I'm fine. I was just tired. Let's finish the goddamn rehearsal."

Tina walked toward him with her EMT bag. "Let me just check your blood pressure again, okay, Mister Caldwell? One thing at a time. How's that sound?"

Caldwell's shoulders sagged. He took a deep breath and exhaled slowly. He stopped working on his tie. He smiled weakly at his wife, and then his heart stopped beating.

In the instant before he collapsed, Jim Caldwell stared at Tina as if she might be able to tell him what was happening. As if she could explain why he was about to crash to the floor. As if she could promise him that he wasn't going to die in Tommy Blaine's hallway.

Tina felt as if her own heart were about to explode as she raced to his side. She ripped open his shirt and loosened the damn tie that had been so important to him.

52

Dennis was a step behind her. "Okay, I'll take over, Tina. We need to get him to West Plains, ASAP."

Dennis knelt down beside Caldwell. He didn't bother checking for a pulse. He gave him two breaths and then started the chest compressions. Caldwell had a huge chest and Dennis had to put all his weight into the compressions.

Tina turned to Caldwell's wife, who was standing behind her, hands clutched to her mouth. "We need to get him to the hospital. Does the church have a vehicle?"

"A van. They've got a van." She looked over at the minister who was standing over Dennis, like a kid watching at a construction site. "Tommy. Get the van ready. Now!"

The Reverend looked up, startled. "Will do." He turned and ran down the corridor.

"Twenty, twenty-one, twenty-two..." Dennis counted out the compressions. He'd gone through four cycles and there had been no response.

"Dennis, we need to use the defib." Dennis looked up at her. He was close to losing it. "Keep doing CPR. I'll get the machine," she said.

Dennis had finished his training with the biphasic defibrillator last month. Tina's training was to begin next week, but she had assisted Pepe on several calls. She ran back to the parlor and extracted the battery pack, unwound the cables and ran back into the hallway. She knelt down beside Dennis, ready to assist him.

Dennis turned and looked at her. She could see the fear in his eyes. "I can't do it, Tina."

"It's okay. You help me."

He moved over and made room for her. She took the paddles and positioned one paddle on the left side of the chest, at the edge of his ribcage, and the other paddle on the right side of the chest above the nipple.

"Everyone step back," Dennis said. "Okay Tina, I'm setting it for two hundred joules.

Tina held the paddles in place, "Do it," she yelled.

There was a popping sound and Caldwell's limbs twitched, but nothing happened. The hall had started to fill up with the guests who had been waiting in the sanctuary. They were eerily quiet, waiting for Tina and Dennis to perform a miracle. Reverend Blaine ran back up the corridor with a crew from the wedding party.

"I've got the van running," he said.

"Okay, Tina, I'm setting it at two twenty."

Again, no response. Caldwell barely twitched. Procedures called for the second jolt to be at three hundred joules. And with Caldwell's bulk there was a lot of resistance. They needed to be more aggressive.

"Oh my god. Please help him." Paula looked at Tina, her eyes imploring.

"Three hundred, Dennis."

"But—"

"Three hundred now, dammit."

He turned the dial. This time the shock jolted Caldwell's whole body, but there was no response.

"Three-sixty," she yelled.

"He's gone, Tina," Dennis said.

"Goddammit, Dennis." She pushed him aside and turned the dial to three hundred sixty joules. She punched the button. His body bounced again, but the screen still showed his heartbeat function arrhythmic. She waited for the battery pack to recharge. It was hopeless, but she couldn't stop. She turned the dial to the maximum setting. The shock seemed to lift Caldwell off the ground. He opened his eyes.

The scope showed a regular heartbeat.

"Jim!" Paula screamed.

He turned his head to the sound. He blinked and he looked like he was trying to figure out what all the fuss was about.

Tina jumped up. "Take his feet," she said to Dennis. She turned to the minister and his crew. "Three on each side, on my signal, lift." As the men hoisted Caldwell she patted him on the shoulder, "You're doing great, Jim. Just take it easy."

The guests scattered as the scrum wound its way down the corridor to the waiting van. They eased Caldwell on to the carpeted van floor. His wife crawled in next to him and cradled him in her arms. Dennis stood outside the van, his face grim. Tina grabbed him by the shirt and made him look at her. "Call the Highway Patrol. Get us an escort to West Plains."

"Okay." He reached into his pocket and retrieved his cellphone. He nodded to her to indicate that the phone was ringing. "Go ahead. You don't need me."

Five minutes later, with the Reverend driving like a man on a mission, they were back on Route 60 heading south toward Lutheran General Hospital. Tina propped herself up against the wheel well as Paula held her husband's hand and stroked his cheek. She was smiling through her tears. Tina envied them.

She stared out the window at the overcast Missouri sky. The sun had set and there were no stars or moon to show the way. She looked at her watch. It was later than she thought.

THE LOVEBOX

A cleaning lady had found Kazuko's mother face down at her desk, right hand clutching the legal brief she had just marked up. The doctor said she died instantly. A blood clot from her heart broke loose and blocked the artery to her brain. Her mother had a good heart, but Kazuko wasn't sure it could kill her brain. That seemed unlikely.

The partners waited a respectful four weeks before they asked Kazuko's father if he would remove her mother's personal effects from her office. It was, after all, a coveted corner suite with a cherry parquet floor and a view of Times Square. When Kazuko arrived from LaGuardia her father was sitting on the office floor. Three knee-high stacks of legal folders surrounded him.

"Ah, you made it," he said as he scrambled to his feet. "Come in, Doctor." With arms opened wide, he walked across the room to greet her. He looked better than he had a month ago. His blue eyes were clear, and he was back to his English professor corduroys and his comfortably frayed button-down shirt.

As she hugged her father, she detected a faint aroma of cherry tobacco, even though he had given up the pipe long ago. When she was a little girl she would play in her father's study while he worked on his poems and sucked on that pipe, filling the room with a cloying, sweet incense. Kazuko would arrange a tea party and wait for her mother to come home from work. Her mother loved tea parties. Her father would always let her wait up no matter how late it was, but most nights she fell asleep and when she awoke her mother would be gone again.

"Why don't you work on the desk, while I go through these files?" her father said as he settled back on the floor.

Kazuko perched on the edge of her mother's desk chair. The seat cushion had no spring left, and the shiny leather upholstery was cracked and worn. She remembered her mother, long flowing black hair already streaked with gray, hunkered down in that chair so intent on her documents she did not notice the colorful mural little Kazuko had crayoned on the parquet floor.

The desk was mostly empty, but in one compartment, squeezed behind an ancient electronic calculator, Kazuko found a lacquered jewelry box with an ivory samurai on the lid. It had three drawers. She opened the top drawer and smiled.

"Look, Dad. She saved my drawings."

Her father glanced up from his pile. "Ah yes, from your early crayola period." He squinted at the picture of a stick-figure girl with curly black hair and an upraised fist. "That little girl looks angry."

"Passionate, not angry," Kazuko said. She opened the middle drawer and pulled out a rubber-banded packet of letters. Kazuko recognized her father's handwriting. "You must have written these when you were in grad school," she said. She handed them to her father.

He glanced at the packet and then quickly dropped them into his canvas satchel and grabbed another folder – his face inscrutable as he thumbed through the papers.

"Aren't you going to read them?"

He shook his head. "I know what they say."

"Daddy!"

"Maybe later. Not now."

Kazuko opened the bottom drawer. "Ballet slippers?"

Her father dropped the papers and walked over to the desk. "Her toe shoes. Of course." He closed his eyes and rubbed their smooth worn surface against his cheek. "When she danced everything was right with the world." His eyes were shiny as he handed the shoes back to Kazuko.

"Why did she give it up?" she asked.

He knelt down to pick up another folder. "She didn't give it up. She just put it away." He flipped through the file and then jammed it into the wastebasket. "That's what she did with the things she loved."

THIS TRAIN MAKES ALL THE STOPS

H ank knew where to stand. He had commuted on the Red Line for thirty years. When he boarded the train at Monroe Street he got prime position in the middle of the car, away from the crush of sweaty commuters who crammed together at the entrance. It was mid-July and the CTA's air conditioning had given up.

In his former life he would have been schlepping his battered sample case and wearing his wool suit and white shirt with a tie Arlene would have bought for him at Fields or Saks. He would have been thinking about the sales calls he'd made and his plans for the rest of the week, and he would have tried not to think about Arlene waiting at home for him, ready to unload a day's worth of her complaints. The passengers would be packed hip-to-hip and ass-to-ass, and Hank's teeth would be clenched as the train screeched and clattered down the track, and he'd be suffocating from the tang of cheap after-shave and smoke-breath and the international potpourri of BO. And with all that stink and heat and humidity and noise Hank would have been happy.

He gripped the stainless steel loop on the back of a seat occupied by a trim, dark-haired woman who was reading an Elmore Leonard novel. Hank liked everything about her: her taste in literature, her lack of an iPod, the way her silk blouse draped her breasts—which Hank was studiously not staring at—her crooked mouth, the way her eyes darted from side to side as she read, and her smooth skin, which was sort of peach-colored, like she did stuff outside on the weekends. She was pretty, but not too pretty and she was younger than Hank, but not too young. Maybe she was one of those "life possibilities" his employment counselor had been talking about.

Hank's left hand clutched the glossy brochure the CareerFinders counselor had handed him at the end of their session. The brochure, he was told, was full of important stuff he would need as he "pivoted" (the counselor's word) toward his new career (whatever that was going to be). But it didn't have the weight of his old briefcase, and when the train lurched out of the station, Hank lost his balance and fell hard into the tattooed kid standing next to him. The boy grabbed Hank to keep him from tumbling to the floor.

"You okay?" he asked.

Hank steadied himself and he could feel the color rising in his cheeks. He used to be able to hold his satchel in one hand and flip through the Tribune with the other. He nodded at the boy. "Thanks," he said.

When the train pulled into Grand, he couldn't avoid his reflection in the window. His hair was completely gray now. Arlene probably would have told him he looked distinguished, but with the harsh lighting he looked almost frail. He missed Arlene's meals. His polo shirt hung loose and the collar was frayed. Arlene never would have let him leave the house looking like that.

This time, as the train accelerated, he held on tight. The woman had closed her book and was staring at him as though she knew him. Her eyes were friendly, inviting conversation. He would ask her about the book. Let her know he had read it, that they had something in common. And he wouldn't do all the talking. He'd listen to what she had to say and then...

She tugged on his sleeve. "Would you like my seat, sir?" she asked.

Her words crumbled him. He shook his head. "I'm okay," he mumbled. He tried to stand a little straighter, but his strength was gone. As the train screeched to a stop at Clark & Division his hand nearly slipped from the handhold. The man seated next to the woman got off and she moved over to the window seat. Hank dropped himself into the seat next to her. He sighed deeply.

"Long day?" she said, again smiling.

"Not long. Just different." He looked at the brochure. He snorted. "My future is behind me," he said.

"Behind you?" she said, her eyebrows peaked.

"A sportscaster once proclaimed of some hotshot rookie that, 'most of his future is ahead of him.'" He shook his head. "Most of my future isn't."

She tilted her head to read the cover of the CareerFinders brochure. "You're looking for a new job?" she asked.

"I'm looking for an old job. But they don't make them anymore. I was in printing services--you know, company newsletters, handbooks, brochures. Arlene warned me. Told me the internet would make me obsolete. What do you do?" he asked.

"I'm a librarian."

Hank raised his eyebrow.

"We're not obsolete. Not yet," she said. "But we've had to adapt."

"Yeah that's what Arlene always told me. 'You've got to retrain, Hank. Go to trade school, Hank. Upgrade yourself, Hank.'"

The train emerged from underground. In the natural light he could see friendly lines around her eyes.

"My name's Hank," he said.

She smiled. A southbound train roared past the window. "I'm Diane," she said, after the clamor subsided.

They rolled past familiar landscapes: Treasure Island and Torstenson Glass Company and the dog park and then the backside of a row of Chicago-brick three-flats.

"See that guy there?" Hank said. He pointed out the window where an old man was seated in a folding chair on the third-floor stoop drinking a beer.

"He looks content," Diane said. The train started to slow for the Fullerton stop.

Hank leaned forward. "When the train slows down, I can look into those apartments and watch people having dinner or reading a book or washing dishes. I imagine their lives."

The conductor announced the transfers for Belmont. Diane leaned toward him to make room for a large woman making her way to the exit. "Is Arlene your wife?" she asked.

He nodded. Nobody ever asked him about Arlene anymore. "She died last year. Breast cancer," he said.

She touched his forearm, just for an instant. "I'm sorry."

"We were married for twenty-one years and Arlene was a complete pain-in-the-ass for nineteen of those years."

Diane laughed and then quickly covered her mouth. "I guess sometimes marriage changes people."

Hank shook his head. "Arlene was always in my corner, but she was annoying when I met her and she just got worse after we were married. Complained about everything—the weather, neighbors, politicians. Democrat or Republican—didn't matter to Arlene—she was an equal opportunity complainer."

Diane looked at him, the lines around her eyes a little more crinkled. "So what were the two good years?"

"When Arlene got sick her attitude changed. Through all that suffering she never complained. Even developed a sense of humor. Woman was amazing." His voice had turned husky. More passengers exited at Belmont. The aisle was now empty. "Dying," Frank said. "That was Arlene's finest moment."

Diane squeezed his hand. "When I get home I'm not going to complain to my boyfriend about anything," she said. "Unless he really screws up."

Of course she had a boyfriend. Hank should have expected that.

The train doors whooshed open and the computer-voiced conductor announced they'd arrived at Addison. Diane shoved her book into her bag. "This is my stop."

As she stood, Hank tapped her on the arm. "Just remember. Most of your future's ahead of you," he said. They laughed.

Her eyes crinkled. "So is yours, Hank."

When she got to the train door she turned and gave him a little wave. Hank couldn't help but smile. He had liked everything about her. Well, everything except for the boyfriend thing. As they pulled out of the station he watched the sun-washed neighborhoods roll by.

LETTING GO

T he clock in the West Plains Lutheran General emergency room has a white face with large black numerals. It's easy to read, like the clocks Paula remembers from grade school. The time is eight twenty-three. Below the clock are swinging double doors, their sickly green exterior scuffed and pockmarked. Seven minutes ago they wheeled her husband through those doors.

A doctor will soon come through those doors. A Missouri country doctor with a rumpled lab coat (stethoscope hanging from one of the pockets) and a tangle of grey hair. Flashing a toothy smile, hands on hips, he'll tell Paula the big guy just had a bad case of indigestion. Take him home and he'll be fine for your daughter's wedding tomorrow. Just make sure he goes easy on the wedding toasts, he'll say. And then he'll wink.

Or the message will come from a young resident with close-cropped hair and sparkling blue eyes. Full of himself, still not quite believing he's a doctor, he'll bust through the doors and inform Paula (and the rest of the waiting room) that they were lucky this time. He'll clear his throat and proclaim that Mr. Caldwell suffered a panic attack. Then he will furrow his brow and continue his lecture. Your husband must go on a strict diet, he will say. He will emphasize "your husband" as though it's her fault Jim weighs two hundred and ninety-seven pounds.

Or they'll usher Paula into a room where there will be some foreign doctor from Pakistan or Ghana waiting for her. A surgical mask will hang loose around his neck and his face will be pinched, as if his stomach hurts. He will stare at his shoes as he tells her he's sorry. And Paula will try to scream, but she won't be able to make a sound.

Paula perches on the edge of her chair and tries to not look down at her dress. When Jim collapsed to the floor just before the wedding rehearsal was about to begin, he broke his nose. The Maple Springs ambulance was unavailable so after that woman EMT resuscitated Jim, the Reverend Tommy Blaine drove Jim and Paula and the EMT to the hospital in West Plains twenty miles away. Tommy had been magnificent, driving the church van like a man possessed. Paula had held Jim's head in her lap and now the silk dress she bought at Dillards, a shimmering periwinkle with a cinched waist that accentuated her trim figure, is dotted with his blood.

She fumbles through her purse and grabs her cellphone. There is a message from her daughter, Kayla. She and Barry are on the way to the hospital

– Jim's brother Clark is driving them. Hearing Clark's name always gives Paula a tight feeling in her stomach. She drops the cellphone back in her purse and retrieves her compact. The whites of her eyes are splashed with a fuzzy redness and her short dark hair is clumpy as though she has just finished a workout.

The double-doors swing open and the EMT who resuscitated her husband, emerges. Trixie or Tina, Paula can't remember her name, takes one of the plastics chairs and turns it so it's at a right angle to Paula's. She whispers, "They're giving him an EKG and they've paged Dr. Khan, he's the cardiologist on-call tonight." She pats Paula's knee. "Where did your minister go?"

"He had a call on his cell."

The woman doesn't look like an EMT to Paula. Fortyish, maybe younger. Hard to tell with her pixie hairstyle and smooth unlined face. She's tanned and has muscular arms and is wearing cutoffs and a white peasant blouse that leaves her midriff bare. Paula had expected a crew of uniformed medical professionals, like on television, but the emergency call was answered by the Maple Springs Volunteer Fire Department. This woman might have been at some bar when she got the call.

Paula tries to read the woman's name on the plastic ID badge she has hooked to her cutoffs. "Thank you for everything." She touches her forearm. "I'm sorry. I've forgotten your name."

"Tina Bennett," she says. Tina stands up and moves her chair next to Paula's and then sits down again. "I'll wait with you."

The glass double doors of the pedestrian entrance fly open. A young hillbilly couple stand in the entrance with their infant wrapped up in a blanket. The admitting nurse, a freckle-splashed redhead, grabs the bundle from the mother and rushes through the double doors.

"What's going on?" Paula asks.

Tina is staring at the couple who stumble to the corner of the waiting room like survivors from a train wreck. "Their baby is dead," she says.

The room goes quiet as two West Plains police officers appear out of nowhere. The older one, who is short and has grey hair and a paunch, takes off his hat and wipes his brow. He ambles over to the nurse at the check-in podium. His partner, who is in his early twenties and tall with a flat belly and broad shoulders, stands in the doorway. His walkie-talkie squawks and a woman's voice asks him to copy. The officer at the podium listens to the redheaded nurse, and then turns to his partner and tilts his head toward the couple in the corner. The younger officer holsters his walkie-talkie and walks over to them.

Tommy Blaine enters the waiting room, flips his cellphone shut and slips it into the front pocket of his Dockers. He does a quick hand-comb, even though he has had a buzz-cut ever since he became the senior pastor. He scans the waiting room from right to left and then back again.

He does the same things on Sundays when he preaches. He avoids the pulpit and stands in the middle of the sanctuary so he can make eye contact with the congregation. He is young, barely thirty, and his eyes, a faded blue like comfortable jeans, are his weapon.

Three summers ago he stood at the church entrance after his "Feed My Sheep" sermon and greeted each member of the congregation as they filed out. When it was Paula's turn, he smiled and clasped her hand. His grip was firm but gentle, and he didn't let go with his hands or his eyes. He invited her to join his Meals on Wheels Ministry and without hesitation she said yes. With Tommy's vision and Paula's hard work they built the program. In the last twelve months the Meals on Wheels Ministry of Maple Springs delivered nine hundred and fifty hot meals to shuts-in and the elderly throughout the county.

As Paula watches him standing there in the middle of the waiting room she wants to believe that what she feels when she sees Tommy is the warmth of Jesus' love shining on her through Tommy. Now that's she's been Born Again, she wants to believe that the flushed feeling in her cheeks and the tingling in her loins are not symptoms of the lust she remembers from her days as a sinner, but something different. Something pure and good and decent. She wants to believe this, but she doesn't.

Even now, with poor Jim fighting for his life, Paula is aware that her heart blips and her breathing is self-conscious as she waits for Tommy to discover her. When he sees her he smiles and she feels unreasonably happy to be noticed. As he approaches, Tommy opens his arms wide, but then he spots Tina and the spell is broken. He assumes his divinity school, concerned-pastor face.

"How is James doing?" he asks Tina.

Paula answers for her. "We don't know yet." She doesn't recognize the sound of her own voice. It's harsh, brittle.

The country boy jumps to his feet as the officer approaches. He nods and they walk out the door together. Tommy peers through the window as they take a seat on the bench in front of the driveway. "What do the police want with that young man?"

Paula watches the boy cover his face with his hands. "They brought their baby in, but Tina says it was already dead."

Tommy closes his eyes. The woman starts to moan. "She needs help. Excuse me, ladies."

Paula wants to grab hold of him. She wants to tell him not to leave her. She wants to tell him she needs him more than that sad little girl with the dead baby. She wants to say, Hold me Tommy, give me faith.

Tommy is careful and deliberate as he approaches the woman, as though she were a stray dog running wild in the neighborhood. He goes down on one knee and holds out his hand as he says something to her. She stops rocking and then she buries her head in his chest, sobbing. He wraps his arms around her and strokes her greasy hair.

Paula picks up an old issue of People and slips back into her chair. People proclaims Jude Law to be the sexiest man alive. She tries to read the article, but she can't get through the first paragraph. She throws the magazine back on the table.

Tina takes out her cellphone and makes a call. "Hi Annie. Hope you're being a good girl. I need a ride back from West Plains, so if you get this message, give me a call. Thanks."

"We can give you a ride home, Tina," Paula says. "Jim's brother Clark is on his way here with my daughter. Clark will be glad to help."

"But he won't want to..."

"Trust me. The last thing Clark wants is to be stuck for hours in a waiting room with me."

"Why not?"

Paula shakes her head. She doesn't want to remember the life she led before she met Jim Caldwell. Doesn't want to remember the wild girl who partied with bad-boy Clark and his rowdy friends. She was a different person back then. When she met Jim she gave up all that. Clark tried to talk his brother out of marrying her, but Jim wouldn't listen. He loved her. Clark didn't believe people could change. Not him, not Paula, not anyone. Tommy would tell her a good Christian should show forgiveness and love her enemy, but she didn't hate Clark enough to love him.

Across the room Tommy is ministering to the young woman. Her eyes are closed, her face pinched. Tommy places his hand on her forehead and prays with her. As he delivers his blessing she lets go. She opens her eyes. They are shiny and focused on Tommy. She has lost the vacant zombie-look she had when she arrived.

The public address system squawks to life: Dr. Khan to operating room three, code blue. Dr. Khan to operating room three, code blue. Paula sits up straight and grabs Tina by the arm. "What does that mean? Is that Jim?"

"I don't know."

Paula bites down on her lower lip to keep her teeth from chattering.

Tommy has heard the announcement. He marches across the room, almost colliding with the admitting nurse, and says to Paula, "I'm going to accompany Beth Ann to the police station. She needs to tell them her story."

"Beth Ann? But what about..."

Tommy turns to Tina. "Can you stay with Paula?"

"Of course."

He leans over and gives Paula a quick hug. "I'll be back soon."

Paula twists away from him and stands up.

"Go. I'm fine." She brushes past him and waits at the podium for the nurse to get off the phone. Out of the corner of her eye, she can see Tommy, with his arm around the girl, walk out the door to the police car parked at the curb.

The nurse doesn't have any new information on Jim. Paula takes a deep breath and walks carefully back to Tina. Her legs feel like jello. She drops into her seat, puts her feet up on the table, and buries her head in her knees. Tina rubs her back.

"I fucking hate men," Paula says.

"Me too. They suck."

Paula lifts her head and peeks at Tina, and they both burst out laughing.

"Oh God, we shouldn't laugh in here."

"Is that another of Tommy's prayers?"

This time Paula laughs so hard she gets hiccups, which follow each laugh like an exclamation point. The hiccups dissolve into sobs.

Tina resumes rubbing her back. "It's okay, Paula. Just breathe in and out. Nice and easy."

"Ah. Those cleansing breaths. I haven't used those since Kayla was born."

"I think it cured your hiccups."

"Better than it worked on childbirth. Are you married, Tina?"

"No."

Paula nods.

"Thanks," Tina says.

"For what?"

"For not giving me that look like I have some terminal disease because I don't have a husband or for not asking me if I'm a lesbian."

Paula looks Tina up and down.

"What?"

"You're not, are you?" she asks. And then she laughs.

Tina laughs too. "No, I've just got really lousy timing. By the time I was ready to get married all the good ones were taken."

Paula leans back and exhales. "Jim and I were just kids when we got married. We didn't know anything about each other. We used to talk for hours. Now, we hardly have to say a word. We're like those chess-playing computers that know your move before you make it," She clasps her hands together like she's praying. "I love him. I really do."

"Sounds like there's a 'but' coming."

"He doesn't make me feel like..."

"Tommy?"

Paula drops her head and stares at the floor. The tile is white with little red and blue specks, the same pattern Tommy selected for the church kitchen when it was remodeled last year. "God, am I that obvious?" she whispers.

"Maybe a little obvious."

Tina smiles at her and Paula takes another deep breath. "When I'm talking with Tommy, my heart starts fluttering and my face feels like it's on fire. I'm like a high school girl. I can barely breathe."

Tina squeezes Paula's hand. She has a comfortable grip. Her hand feels warm and dry. "There's nothing wrong with wanting, Paula."

"I realized something when I saw Jim lying on the floor." Paula looks up as the entrance doors swing open and a large black woman with her teenage daughter enter the waiting room and cautiously approach the podium. "I don't want Tommy. I just want that feeling."

Paula remembers the first time they made love. They were in the backseat of his Chevelle, and Jim's sweaty body pressed her into the bristly green upholstery. She could smell stale cigarette butts from the door-handle ashtray above her head, and she could see the look of pure adoration on Jim's face, as though he were the luckiest man alive, as though she were something special.

She remembers Jim teaching Kayla to ride her bike. An impossibly hot summer day with the kind of humidity that sucked all the oxygen out of the air. Jim, his face a shade beyond red, guided Kayla up and down their long driveway until it finally all came together and she rode out of his grasp and down the country road. Jim stood there at the end of the driveway, his shirt soaked with sweat, one beefy arm raised in triumph and the other waving tentatively as though he were uncertain whether to wave good-bye or reel her back in.

Paula remembers Jim's eyes after he collapsed. He stared up at her with a lost and frightened look that broke her heart. He wanted to know why he was dying on the floor of Tommy Blaine's church, but she couldn't tell him.

The clock in the West Plains Lutheran General emergency room reads nine twenty-seven. The rehearsal dinner would be almost over now. Jim Caldwell would be tapping his water glass and preparing to deliver his toast.

The freckle-splashed redheaded nurse appears out of nowhere. She clutches her clipboard.

"Mrs. Caldwell?"

"Yes?"

"Would you come with me please?"

They leave her in an empty exam room. The room is cold and smells like nail polish remover. Paula shivers. She waits. The door flies open and a young doctor, an Indian or Pakistani, enters. He looks tired, and his surgical mask hangs loose around his neck. His face is pinched, his lips pressed tight. He has kind eyes.

Paula wants to scream, but she doesn't. She waits. Waits for this stranger to deliver the news that will change her life forever.

"Mrs. Caldwell?"

"Yes."

"We moved your husband to the ICU. You may see him now. But just a short visit, okay? He needs to rest."

There are twelve beds in the West Plains Lutheran General Intensive Care Unit. The ICU has all of the latest technology. Twenty-four hour cardiac and arterial pressure monitoring. Intra-venous thrombolysis, fluid, electrolyte and drug management. Airway and mechanical ventilation management. With all this high-tech management how could they not save her husband's heart?

He will be in the bed next to the window, with the view of the parking lot and the Denny's across the street. When she walks into the room he will smile. It won't be the 'howdy partner' smile, but that special smile he reserves just for her. The shy smile of the boy who loved her when she had no right to be loved. The boy whose heart was always true.

There will be tubes and wires and electrodes connected to all parts of his body and the ding and ping and whoop of all that management will make it impossible to talk privately. But she will hold his hand and she will try very hard not to cry. She will whisper in his ear that she has always loved him and always will. And he will give her hand a little squeeze and say, I know, Paula, I know. Me too. And then he will close his eyes.

Praise for Len Joy's

American Past Time

"This darkly nostalgic story is a study of an American family through good times and bad, engagingly set against major events from the 1950s to the '70s as issues of race simmer in the background...an expertly written examination of the importance of dreams to the human psyche.

A well-crafted novel that will particularly appeal to sports and history aficionados."

Kirkus Reviews

"Len Joy has an eye for the humble, utterly convincing details of family life: the look, feel, taste, and smell of work and school, meals and sport. This is mid-twentieth-century America seen neither through the gauze of nostalgia nor with easy cynicism but rather with a clear-eyed tenderness. Readers will care deeply, as I did, about the Stonemasons's inextricable triumphs and failures."

Pamela Erens – author of *The Virgins*

"Here is a "baseball novel" that transcends sport and offers an in-depth portrait of a family and an era.

The novel begins in Dancer Stonemason's perspective but later moves to his wife's and son's perspectives and the effect allows their perceptions and understandings to bump against each other, complicating ideas of truth and love. The scenes are well-drawn and well-edited, filled with dialogue that reads like spoken word (a feat!) and characters who are as complex as real people, with the same complex desires, anger, sadness, and hope as real people as well.

Themes of race, family, father-son relationships are present... But for me the most poignant moment happens near the end when a scene related to the end of the Vietnam War echoes against our present moment. Len Joy does write about a Past Time in America's history, but everything he details feels prescient now."

Kristiana Kahakauwila – author of *This is Paradise*

"...in Len Joy's nostalgic and moving first novel American Past Time, we follow the Stonemason family through the better part of three decades, exploring the unpredictable influences that family, society, and responsibility exert on one's life choices. In this impressive debut, Joy deftly and emotionally explores the many ways in which our relationships, hopes, and dreams can alter the course of our lives."

Mary Akers – author of *Bones of an Inland Sea*

"American Past Time is not only a baseball lovers' novel but one that history buffs will enjoy as well. Through a narrative voice reminiscent of times gone by, it covers the changing social structure in 20th Century America including racial tensions, Vietnam, and parenthood. Men of all ages will love this book."

Eileen Cronin – author of *Mermaid: A Memoir of Resilence*

"An all-American story that goes beyond the scope of the domestic and into the realm of history. A very engaging read."

Chinelo Okparanta – author of *Happiness, Like Water*

"I finished this book some weeks ago and wanted to wait to review it, to see if the story stayed with me. So many books I initially love I don't remember much about weeks or even days later.

This book held up. I've been thinking about why. It's not a hurtling read, nor is the writing so innovative your mind shatters. It's got baseball in it, and I hate baseball. However, the story is so clearly and simply told--the book doesn't get in the way of itself at all, and what you're left with is a clean-lined beauty. There's nothing extraneous, nothing sentimental, even though there are emotional moments. This book follows a family through the 50s and into near-contemporary times. One review I saw said that it was a good book for "history buffs," but I disagree. Okay, it might be fine for history buffs, but really it's a clear and poignant portrait of a time not only in American life, but in the life of a certain class of people. Working class people, lower middle class people. Many people of my parents' generation, who grew up with relatively simple aspirations. Dancer Stonemason, the father in this family, is the most ambitious of anyone we see closely, in that he has long-shot career goals... to pitch in the major leagues. Otherwise, it's a matter of raising a family, paying a mortgage on a modest house, getting your kids through high school and maybe college. These are humble but dignified people living through a period of enormous social and economic change, including the Civil Rights movement. Even though my parents aren't midwesterners or southerners, I felt I gained a window into their pre-me lives and expectations of their futures. None of which went the way people of that generation expected. This is about regular people, living in a small town yet nonetheless immersed in a larger social context that causes challenges for their daily lives. They work through it, over the course of decades, and so the book has a nice resolution without the reader having to feel hit over the head with THIS IS A RESOLUTION."

Claudia Putnam – author of *Wild Thing in Our Known World*

"Len Joy's American Past Time is a wonderful debut. Its protagonist, Dancer Stonemason, is a lifelong Midwesterner trying to live out his dreams as a pitcher in the St. Louis Cardinals organization. But with a growing family and an arm that no longer cooperates, plans change.

Told against the backdrop of the "idyllic" 50's and "turbulent" 60's, Joy's compelling prose and exceptional characters take the reader through an intriguing period in American history."

Roland Goity – editor of *WIPs: Works in Progress*

"Life is a series of choices, a series of dreams, each impacting the dynamics of relationships in complex ways.

Set in the 1950s--1970s, this historical novel about a complicated family impacted by the father's decisions and dreams is fast paced, clearly written and quite relevant. Bits of history are ambient reminders of what era the reader has been submerged into. The civil rights movement, memorable baseball names and moments, pop culture of the 1960s, Vietnam war. Len gets under the skin of his characters and succeeds in placing the reader right there-- in the small town world of high school games and minor league baseball, the heated drudgery of the foundry, the smokey filled bars, the blue collar culture. I felt that I was right there in the middle of it all.

Don't miss this book. Easy to buy, easy to read. You'll finish it fast because you won't want to leave these characters."

Debbie Ann Eis – author of *Lament for the Coons*

"The story was set against a backdrop of a number of major events in American history, such as the moon landing, the Vietnam war, the assassination of Kennedy, etc.

This was most definitely one of those books that I did not want to end. I found myself always wanting to know what happened next to the characters. I would have been happy had the book been double the length.

I would recommend this book to, well, just about anyone really. I enjoyed this immensely."

Julian Froment book review blog

"...a timeless classic."

Jersey Girl Book Reviews

Len Joy lives in Evanston, Illinois.

His first novel, AMERICAN PAST TIME, was published in 2014. Kirkus Reviews called it "a well-crafted novel and a darkly nostalgic study of an American family through good times and bad."

He is a nationally ranked triathlete and a member of TEAM USA, representing the USA in international triathlon competition.

89073185R00052

Made in the USA
Middletown, DE
14 September 2018